London Art Chase

Other books by Natalie Grant

Glimmer Girls series

A Dolphin Wish (Book Two)

faithgirlz

London Art Chase

by Natalie Grant
with Naomi Kinsman

ZONDERkidz™

ZONDERKIDZ

London Art Chase
Copyright © 2016 by Natalie Grant
Illustrations © 2016 by Cathi Mingus

This title is also available as a Zondervan ebook.
Visit www.zondervan.com/ebooks

Requests for information should be addressed to:
Zonderkidz, 3900 Sparks Drive, Grand Rapids, Michigan 49546

ISBN 978-0-310-75265-3

Art direction: Cindy Davis
Cover design and interior illustrations: Cathi Mingus
Content contributor: Naomi Kinsman
Interior design: Denise Froehlich

Printed in the United States of America

16 17 18 19 20 21 22 23 24 25 /DCI/ 15 14 13 12 11 10 9 8 7 6 5 4 3 2 1

To my glimmer girls—Gracie, Bella, and Sadie.
You're my greatest adventure. I love you.

ACKNOWLEDGMENTS

Thank you to Naomi Kinsman for bringing your genius creativity and beautiful patience to this process. None of this would be a reality without you.

ONE

A clothes tornado had struck, sweeping Maddie, Mia, and Lulu right along with it. Hats, shoes, T-shirts, skirts, jeans, sweaters, coats, and even a feather boa or two were strewn across Maddie's bedroom. Piles spilled over the edges of their suitcases and covered the floor, topped here and there with various dolls from Lulu's collection, Maddie's sketchbook and colored pencils, and Mia's endless collection of books.

"Girls, what in the world . . . ?"

One look at Miss Julia's face and Maddie burst out laughing. Even without checking, she knew Mia was laughing too. Topping the list of what she loved about being a twin was this—the way she and Mia could almost always read each other's minds. A close second was the way she and Mia fit together, like the chords and melody of a song. Mia was only three minutes older, but she was also three inches taller and three times faster to know the just-right thing to say. Mia always had a plan, but Maddie was the one who'd convince Lulu to play along. Plus, Maddie could stop any argument between her twin and her little sister in its tracks.

"We're picking the most London-y things we can find!" Lulu announced, throwing her arms around their nanny in a giant hug. "Come and see!"

Miss Julia hugged Lulu back. "It looks to me like you've picked everything in your closets!"

Mia's eyes lit up the way they always did when she had a new plan. "I know! Let's have a fashion show. Miss Julia, you can help us pick our outfits."

"Mommy said we could choose first, and then she'd check our suitcases to make sure we had everything we need," Lulu said.

"Everything you need, plus a princess dress?" Miss Julia teased.

"We're going to see a palace, so I definitely need my princess dress." Lulu fished her crown out of the pile and placed it on her head. "*And* this, of course."

"Did I hear something about a fashion show?" Mom asked as she came up the stairs.

Her eyes went wide as she took in the disaster that used to be Maddie's room.

"Mom," Maddie said, catching Mia's eye. "You should be in our fashion show too. We can go in your closet and help you choose perfect outfits for your concerts."

"Gloria Glimmer . . . sporting her princess finest," Dad called up from the kitchen.

Mom winked at Maddie. "Nice try, kiddo, but after seeing this room, I'm not letting the three of you any-where near my closet. I'd love to watch your fashion show, though."

"Go sit on the couch. And close your eyes. And count to 100," Lulu said.

"Wait!" Mia said. "We should make a list of all the places we're going. We're going to the palace, right?

"Yes, and to the Tower of London," Mom said.

"What's that?" Lulu asked.

"At the Tower of London, there's a room where you'll see jewelry and crowns that belonged to real princesses and queens."

Mia picked her way across the mess and returned with a notebook and pencil. "Okay, so the palace and the Tower of London, and what else?"

"We'll see art, won't we?" Even though Maddie already knew the answer, she had to ask again.

"Exactly. You'll go to the National Gallery of Art, where they have every kind of painting, plus a gallery where kids can make their own art too. And we'll see cathedrals and Big Ben—"

"Who's Big Ben?" Lulu asked.

"Remember the clock in *Peter Pan*?"

"Ooh, will we see him too?" Lulu clapped her hands.

"Lulu, you know Peter Pan's not real," Mia said.

Lulu opened her mouth to argue, but Maddie jumped in to stop the fight before it started, "Why's the clock called Big Ben?"

"You know, I'm not sure," Mom said.

"It's actually not the clock that's called Big Ben," Miss Julia said, reading off her phone. "Big Ben is the Great Bell inside the tower that chimes—along with a lot of other smaller bells—every quarter hour. Some

11

people think the Great Bell is named after Sir Benjamin Hall because he oversaw its installation. But others think it's named after Benjamin Caunt, England's heavy-weight boxing champion."

"Fashion show time!" Lulu shouted, twirling around in the assortment of clothes she'd been pulling on— shiny purple boots, a fringed skirt, a multicolored, striped T-shirt, and a glittery, hot pink sunglasses.

"We'd better go downstairs," Miss Julia said.

"And close your eyes!" Lulu called after them. "Count to 100."

They'd only reached 40 by the time Maddie, Mia, and Lulu had lined up on the stairs.

"Open your eyes!" shouted Lulu, and then, "WAIT! Keep them closed. Get Daddy to play the piano. We need fashion show music!"

"How are they supposed to keep their eyes closed and get Dad too?" Mia asked.

"Upstairs, upstairs!" said Lulu, pulling her sisters up to the landing.

When Rachmaninoff's Piano Concerto No. 3 wafted up the stairs, the girls sashayed back down again, this time with extra flair to match the music.

"These are our touring-round-town outfits," Mia said. "Including comfortable shoes so we can walk and walk."

Mia was wearing her favorite shoes. Lulu still wore her purple boots. Maddie had shoved her feet into ballet flats after pulling on a skirt and her favorite scarf and jacket. Mia was wearing her favorite T-shirt. It had shooting stars.

"You might want to add an umbrella," Miss Julia said. "And jackets. It rains almost every other day in London, even in June."

"It won't rain for the Glimmer tour," Lulu said. "It will be just lov-e-ly."

After the girls floated up and down the stairs modeling a full range of outfits, Mom and Miss Julia gave them a standing ovation. Then Dad kissed the tops of each of their heads.

"Now, let's finish packing those suitcases," Mom said. "And see if we can find Maddie's floor again before dinner. Deal?"

"Can we have pizza?" Mia asked.

"Barbecue chicken pizza!" Maddie suggested.

"And Doritos?" Lulu added. "And Cheetos and bologna?"

"Maybe pizza," Mom said, eyeing them each in turn. "Plus salad. And maybe, if we get all our packing done, chocolate cookies for dessert."

"Deal!" the girls said in unison before racing each other up to Maddie's room.

TWO

Lulu bounced up and down on her toes as everyone took their luggage down from the overhead bins and slowly filtered out of the airplane. Maddie knew exactly how Lulu felt. All she wanted was to stand someplace where she had space to stretch her arms and legs. Between the flight from Nashville to Washington, D.C., and this flight from D.C. to London, they had watched four movies, eaten breakfast, lunch, and dinner—plus three snacks—and she'd taken two naps. Maddie had read as much of her book as her eyes could bear, had drawn every last thing she could think of in her sketchpad, and even still, she'd run out of things to do almost twenty minutes ago.

Finally, *finally*, the aisle cleared, and Dad led the way out of the airplane. Lulu exploded out of the air bridge into the first empty space she could find and started to twirl and leap. Sometimes Maddie wished she could be six again and get away with things like Lulu did. No one was irritated with her little sister's twirling, not even the businessman she accidentally knocked into. But honestly, even when Maddie was six, she couldn't have ignored the way everyone was watching. Lulu didn't seem to even notice. Maddie stretched her arms and legs, laughing as Dad joined Lulu and helped her twirl. Miss Julia snapped picture after picture.

"Are you making another collage?" Maddie asked, peeking over Miss Julia's shoulder.

"Look at this app," she said, with her familiar burst of enthusiasm about anything new and creative. "I can make Lulu look like she's in a graphic novel, or a black-and-white sketch." She flicked through options. "Which one should we use?"

"I say go with the watercolor-looking one. It's the one that actually looks like Lulu is in motion."

Miss Julia clicked again a few times, finalizing the picture. "Nice choice."

Mom put one arm around Maddie and the other around Mia, pulling them both close. "Are my beautiful girls ready to see London?"

Maddie could tell Mia was wound tight with just as much excitement as she was.

"Yes!" they chimed together.

As they made their way through the airport, the Glimmer family might as well have been a parade. Lulu led the way.

"Come on, guys, this way!" she kept shouting, even though Dad was the one actually reading the signs and making sure they were headed for baggage claim.

Dad didn't always come on tour with Mom. The girls came along most of the time, but Dad had to split his time between touring and arranging and producing music. Mom joked that Dad always found time to tour to exceptional places, like Hawaii for instance, but when she played in Nebraska or Kansas, Dad's other work called. London must fall into the very-fun category, though, because Dad had cleared his schedule. Maddie liked it best when Dad came on tour, first of all because he always made everything more fun. But also because she liked watching him play piano for Mom at concerts. Maddie especially liked the way Mom's eyes lit up when she glanced over at Dad onstage.

"Baggage carousel number five!" Dad announced. "We'll take all the pink and purple suitcases, thank you very much."

The girls laughed as Dad collected their pile of suit-cases, which were—like he said—all pink and purple. His was the exception, gray with orange stripes. When the belt started slowing down, he'd found all of the suit-cases but one.

"Where's my suitcase?" Lulu wailed. "The one with all my toys?"

"I'm sure it's here," Miss Julia said, hurrying around the other side of the carousel.

Everyone looked, but Lulu's pink-striped case was nowhere to be seen.

"My suitcase is gone!" Lulu cried, tears filling her eyes. "My suitcase!"

Maddie wrapped her arms around her sister, hug-ging her tight. "It's okay, Lulu. We'll find it."

Lulu's wails only grew louder. "My suitcase, my suitcase, my suitcase!!"

"Listen, Lulu," Maddie said. "You can share my toys. I'll give you half of what's in my case for the whole trip, okay?"

At this, Lulu's wails quieted, and she looked up at Maddie with watery eyes. "But what if we don't find my toys . . . ever?"

"We'll find your suitcase. I'm sure we will," Maddie said.

Mia came over and joined the hug. "Maybe there's a lost and found."

"Now there's an excellent idea," Miss Julia said, herding the girls toward an official-looking door. "Let's check in the office."

Dad stayed with the luggage cart. Mom went with the girls to talk to the airline officer.

"What happened?" he asked, looking from Lulu's tear-streaked face to the rest of the group.

"We're missing a suitcase," Miss Julia said.

"A pink one with stripes!" Lulu said, her voice rising into an almost-wail all over again.

Maddie rubbed Lulu's back in circles, the way that always helped calm her down.

"Hmm . . ." the man said, furrowing his brow. Maddie could see he really didn't want to disappoint Lulu. "Let me check in the back."

The minute he returned, eyebrows furrowed deep, Maddie knew. The suitcase wasn't there. If only it had been her toy case, or even her clothes . . . anything other than Lulu's toys.

"Why don't you write your hotel's name on this form," he said to Mom. "I'll research where the bag might be, and deliver it myself as soon as we locate it. Where did you have your layover?"

"Washington D.C.," Mom said, writing quickly and passing the paper back to the man.

"You know what?" Maddie said to Lulu, pulling her sister out of the office before she could start wailing again. "Let's get Felicity. You can have her for the whole trip, okay?"

Dad unstacked suitcases so Maddie could pull out her favorite American Girl doll.

Lulu cradled Felicity in her arms. "Really? For the whole trip?"

"Yes, absolutely," Maddie said.

Mia gave Maddie a *nice-thinking* nod. Lulu loved Felicity in particular, because of her long red hair, and also since in all of Felicity's stories she rode horses, something Lulu was hoping she'd get to do very, very soon.

"And they'll find my suitcase sometime?" Lulu asked Mom, tears welling up again.

"You know what, I think we should pray that the suitcase finds its way to us with no trouble at all," Mom said.

"But should we really pray about a suitcase?" Mia asked. "I mean, is a suitcase important enough to pray about? No offense, Lulu," she added quickly.

"God wants to hear about all the things that matter to us," Dad said. "You're right, Mia, we shouldn't treat him like a genie in the sky who grants all our wishes. But praying is just as much for us as it is for God. When we pray, we are reminded that we can trust him with everything, no matter how big or small."

"I'll pray!" Lulu piped up.

"Perfect," Mom said.

Everyone closed their eyes, and Lulu said, "God, I know you're really good at finding stuff, so could you please look for my pink-striped suitcase? When you find it, we'll be at . . . Wait, Mommy, where is our hotel?"

Maddie cracked her eyes open in time to catch Mom's mouth twitch, the faintest hint of a smile. "The Grand at Trafalgar Square."

"Right, what Mommy just said. We'll be staying there. And thank you for taking care of us, and for Mommy and Daddy and Miss Julia and Maddie and Mia and for Felicity too. Amen."

Maddie made a special effort not to look at Mia when she opened her eyes, because she knew they'd both burst out laughing and Lulu wouldn't understand. She bit the corner of her mouth and counted silently until the feeling passed.

"I think it's time to show Felicity her first bit of London," Mom said. "Are we ready?"

"Yes!" the girls all said.

"After you, ladies!" Dad said, gesturing toward the door.

Maddie, Mia, and Lulu linked arms and together led the way out to the streets of London.

THREE

The cab ride to the hotel took almost an hour, but Maddie didn't mind. Everywhere she looked something was completely new and surprising, from the way the driver's wheel was on the wrong side of the car, to the way the cab looked like a giant black beetle, to the way Mom, Dad, and Miss Julia rode in a seat that faced backward toward the girls. They careened through the streets of London. Careening was exactly the right word. Maddie felt more like she was on a roller coaster than in a car as they curved through roundabout after roundabout.

Outside her window, the city flew past, a city that looked like it couldn't exist in this century. Everything was made of stone and marble and iron, and still, every once in a while she'd see something from absolutely right now, like a Starbucks or a person sitting at a bus stop tapping away at a cell phone's glowing screen. The buildings were enormous, decorated with pillars and fancy carved window frames and sometimes even a carved gargoyle or odd face. Every building was topped a different way, with brick chimneys or round domes or spiked towers. The lampposts looked like they belonged in Narnia.

Every twenty seconds or so, Lulu would point out the window and say, "Ooh, look at that!" until no one even knew what she was pointing out at all. No one tried to figure it out, either, because they were busy trying to soak in the sights themselves. Even Mom and Dad oohed and aahed like kids. After a few minutes, Miss Julia stopped looking up every architectural feature on her phone and instead began snapping pictures again.

Mom asked the cabbie to pull up to the curb at Trafalgar Square so they could walk past the statues of lions and the fountain. "Can you circle the square a few times for us, and then pick us up?"

The cabbie agreed, and everyone climbed out of the car.

"It's like traveling in a time machine," Mia said, and then, "Wait, Lulu!"

But Lulu was already sprinting for the closest lion. She'd climbed halfway up by the time the rest of the group caught up with her. Lulu tucked Felicity under her arm and climbed the rest of the way.

"Look at me!" Lulu shouted, balancing herself on the lion's huge bronze back.

"Lulu, you absolutely must stay with us," Mom said. "No running off, no matter what, do you hear me?"

"But, Mommy! I'm riding a lion!"

Mom nudged Maddie and Mia toward the lion. "Might as well go up there and join her so Miss Julia can take some pictures."

Mia helped Maddie up and they sat three in a row, with Felicity in front, all of the girls smiling for the camera. Across the stone square, water shot up into the air and splashed over the sides of the fountain. People crisscrossed from one street to another, some taking photos like the Glimmer family, and others clearly on their way to their offices or important meetings.

"Should we go settle into our hotel?" Mom asked. "The people who brought us in for the concert had a connection to the hotel, and arranged for us to have a very special room."

"I hear there's even a grand piano in our room!" Dad said.

"Does that mean we have to practice while we're here?" Lulu asked, her face falling.

"It means you *get* to practice," Dad said, helping her down off the lion.

"Maddie! A grand piano!" Mia said, eyes dancing. "Race you for first dibs!"

"No one is running off ahead of anyone else," Dad reminded, catching Mia before she could take three steps. "Look, the cabbie is rounding the corner now. Let's go catch him."

"Race you once we're there," Mia whispered in Maddie's ear.

"You're on," Maddie whispered back.

The doorman wore a top hat and a jacket with long tails. He greeted them with a bow and opened the doors. A bellboy loaded their suitcases onto a cart and led them to the front desk.

"Whoa," Lulu said, looking around the lobby with its giant pillars and marble statues. "This is the most lovely hotel I have ever seen!"

Everyone turned to look at Lulu, whose loud, clear voice echoed through the lobby like a bell.

"Why, thank you, miss," the bellboy said, just as loudly, giving Maddie a swift wink.

After Mom and Dad had gathered keys, they piled into the elevator and went up to their rooms. When the bellboy opened the door, Maddie could hardly believe her eyes. With all of the traveling they had done she had been in a lot of hotels in her life, but these rooms were the most amazing she had ever seen.

"Welcome to the Musician's Penthouse," the bellboy said, presenting the room with a flourish.

"Whoa!" Lulu said.

The room had two levels, plenty of bedrooms for everyone—even Miss Julia—and a spiral staircase right in the middle of the first floor. And sure enough, a grand piano sat in the middle of the living room.

Mia flew over to it—the way Maddie knew she would—and lined up her fingers to play. Soon, Pachelbel's Canon filled the room. Maddie crossed to look out the huge windows. She could see Trafalgar Square, Big Ben, and even the river crisscrossed by a few bridges.

"Chocolate!" cried Lulu, causing Mia to stop playing and Maddie to come running.

Sure enough, on the coffee table was a bowl of chocolate truffles. The girls each grabbed one chocolate and then another, knowing that any minute one of the adults would give them a chocolate limit.

It was Miss Julia who laughed and then said, "Okay, okay. Three is enough for now. Let's explore a little more."

Maddie, Mia, and Lulu bounded around the entire penthouse, checking out the bathtub that was big enough to be a hot tub, trying out the little violet and vanilla scented lotions, just-right-sized robes and slippers, and bouncing on every single fluffy bed. Everywhere they looked, huge windows showed off views of London. Lulu decided the overstuffed chair in the girls' room was the perfect resting place for Felicity.

"This is the loveliest hotel room I've ever, ever seen," Lulu said.

"I'm blown away," Mom said. "It's the kind of room royalty would stay in, fit for my three princesses. Girls, we'll have to thank our hosts for giving us such an amazing experience. And we should whisper a special thank you to God in our hearts for blessing us so extravagantly. I have a feeling this is going to be a special trip."

Dad began to play a medley of songs on the piano. Mom curled up on a couch with a magazine, and the girls piled up next to her, one after the other, cuddling close to listen.

After a few songs, Mom said, "We should probably find something to eat."

"I know!" Mia announced. "We're in London, so we should have afternoon tea!"

"That, Mia, is a fabulous idea," Mom said, heading for the girls' room. "And I know just where we can go. Let's see what dresses we can find in those suitcases of yours to wear to tea at the Savoy."

Maddie felt like she'd stepped into a fairy world where she and her sisters had become princesses. So far, this was the very best place Mom had ever taken them on tour.

FOUR

No one wanted to get right back into a cab, so they started walking across Trafalgar Square on foot. Dad gave Lulu a piggyback ride because her shoes were a little too tight.

"Mom, I think you should let us sing in your concert," Mia said.

"Oh you do, do you?" Mom asked, her eyes dancing.

"We could have a special song, like the one you wrote for us. I'll bet the audience would love it."

"Love it, love it, love it!" agreed Lulu.

"And what would your song be about?" Mom asked.

Maddie shuddered. Her palms felt immediately sweaty. Mia often had wild suggestions like this, but Mom usually said no right away. This time, Mom seemed to be considering the idea. Lately, Mia had been having a lot of ideas about performing. Mom had even signed them up for a theater camp. Maddie didn't mind watching Mom on stage, but being up there herself—in front of everyone—would be a completely different situation.

"Maybe we could sing about dreaming big, or something like that. What do you think, Maddie?" Mia asked.

They had just passed through the Trafalgar Square gate. Maddie latched on to the first distraction she saw, a red booth on the corner.

"What's that, Mom?" she asked.

"You mean the telephone booth?" she asked.

"The what?" Mia asked, while Maddie went to take a closer look.

Tossing Mom a grin, Dad set Lulu down. "Here, I'll demonstrate."

He opened the glass-paned door and went inside, picking up the telephone receiver and holding it up to his ear. "Just need a coin, here," he said, rummaging in his pocket. "How many coins does a telephone booth in London take, anyway?

Of course, Miss Julia pulled out her phone. "Google to the rescue!" She scrolled for a moment, frowned, and then scrolled again.

"What does it say?" Lulu asked.

"It's not as simple as you'd think," Miss Julia said. "First of all, the British pound has only followed a decimal system since 1971. So, now, a pound equals 100 pence, but before 1971 a pound equaled 20 shillings, and a shilling equaled 12 pence."

Maddie wrinkled her nose, doing the math in her mind. "So a pound used to be worth 240 pence?"

"That's confusing," Mia said. "No wonder they changed to decimals."

"It's fascinating," Miss Julia said, still scrolling. "They argued over the concept for centuries, and finally decided they had to change in order to be more consistent with the rest of the world. One day—Decimal

Day—they switched, and their entire coin system changed."

"So how much does this telephone booth cost, then?" Dad asked.

"Looks like 60 pence," Miss Julia said. "And that gives you up to 30 minutes for a local or national call."

Dad sorted his coins and then dropped a few into the slot. "Now who should I dial?"

"Wait, so people pay money to make calls in London? Don't they have real phones?" Mia asked.

"Even we have our emergency phones to call Mom or Miss Julia," Maddie said, pulling hers out.

"Before cell phones, public phone booths were the only way to make calls when you were out and about," Mom said.

"Like pay phones back home," Mia said. "I've seen them in movies, I guess, but I can't think of one I've seen in real life. Well, maybe the call boxes on the freeway. I've seen some of those."

"But why is the phone in a booth? And why is the booth so . . . red?" Lulu asked, looking the booth up and down, as though she'd figure it out if she saw it from a different angle.

"Looks like telephone boxes were created by the post office in England." Miss Julia scrolled down her phone screen. "The post office managed mail and telephone, all communication, and they wanted the phone and post boxes to be architecturally pleasing. So they had a competition, and this is what they ended up with. Red, so the booths were easy to spot."

"Will they keep them always?" Mia asked. "I mean, now that everyone has a phone in their pocket?"

"I hope so," Maddie said, taking a turn inside the booth. "It's like a tiny room you'd go inside and then come out in a new place, like Wonderland."

"Where would you want to find yourself, Mads?" Dad asked.

"Right exactly here," she said, without a moment of hesitation. "On my way to tea with everyone."

"Not me!" Mia said. "I mean, I like London and all, but if I could go anywhere, I'd want to go to a magical world with, I don't know . . . maybe unicorns. Or leprechauns!"

"Or Candy World!" Lulu pumped her fist in the air.

"And what would you eat first?" Dad asked.

Lulu ran through her list of candy for Dad. Mia explained her magical world, holding Mom and Miss Julia captive. Sometimes it felt like their ideas and enthusiasm soaked up everyone's attention, leaving Maddie just a little off-center. Up against a magical world, wanting to be here in London with her family didn't seem all that interesting. Maybe she should have said something about princes who turned into frogs or a genie in a bottle.

And there it was again, the question that popped into her mind every once in a while, the one she usually pushed straight back out, but that she couldn't avoid either. *What about me?* If she and Mia were like chords and melody, Mia was for-sure the melody. Which left Maddie to be the chords, the not-so-glimmery, keep-everything-together part of the music. She knew she had her own glimmer, too, but she hadn't quite figured out what it was.

"You okay?" Miss Julia asked, noticing Maddie trailing behind. "Your shoes aren't bothering you, are they?"

"I'm fine." Maddie forced a smile.

No one had done anything wrong, not really, and she hated causing trouble. Plus, if she wanted to be right here, right now, with her family, she should do her best to enjoy herself . . . even if things didn't go exactly her way.

Dad raised his hand to finally hail a cab, and they all climbed in. Off to the Savoy to have tea, and hopefully to start feeling better.

"So . . . what else besides unicorns?" Maddie asked Mia.

Mia launched in, pulling Maddie and Lulu into the brainstorm, and by the time they pulled up to the curb outside the Savoy they'd created a full-blown magical world complete with cotton candy clouds, glitter fairies, and fences made of daisies.

FIVE

The tables were topped with crisp white cloths, daisies in crystal vases, and more silverware and plates than Maddie had ever seen set out together at the same time. What were all of those forks for? Instead of formal chairs, each table was surrounded by comfy chairs and couches.

Maddie scooted across the couch to make room for Mia and Lulu, careful not to knock into anything. Between her dress and the tablecloth and the couch, she was worried something would pull or snag or trip her up, but in the end, everyone settled in without disaster—even Lulu.

"Dad, you're definitely the only boy in here," Mia said, giggling.

Lulu bounced up and down on the cushion, trying to get a better look around the room. "No other boys at all?"

Dad glanced around the dining room. Then he snapped his napkin like a flag before tucking it into his collar. "If I'm turning in my man card for this little outing, I might as well do it right."

The waitress half-smiled as she passed out the menus, but Maddie could tell she'd have laughed at Dad's napkin if she was allowed. This was something Maddie had noticed about London so far. People seemed to live by a code of rules, one that Maddie didn't see very often back home. For instance, the front desk staff and bellboy at the hotel all spoke very properly, had perfect posture, and mostly wore serious expressions along with their official uniforms. When they smiled, their smiles seemed like mischief, as though they might be breaking some unspoken rule. In Maddie's opinion, the mischief made every smile all the more fun.

"All of our afternoon teas are served with pots of tea, sandwiches, cookies, and scones, but we have a few different options," the waitress said. "You can share pots of tea, or each have your own. I'll give you a moment to look over the menu."

Maddie had no idea which kind of tea she would like. Jasmine? English Rose?

"We should do the classic high tea," Mom said. "With tea sandwiches and sweets too. We can share a few pots of tea so you girls can try a few varieties."

"What kind of sandwiches?" Lulu asked. "Bologna?"

"Well, there's ham and cheese," Mom said. "And egg salad, and of course cucumber and cream cheese. And clotted cream with scones."

"My favorite!" said Miss Julia.

"Clotted cream?" Mia asked. "Like rotten cream, you mean?"

Mom smiled. "Clotted cream is delicious. You'll love it, Mia, I promise."

When the waitress came back, Mom chose a few different kinds of tea. Soon, they had fancy teapots steeping tea on the table, next to tiered silver trays topped with sandwiches and treats.

"I'm going to have a mini cupcake first," Lulu said.

"All right, but a sandwich afterward, okay?" Mom said.

Mia grimaced as she took her first bite of sandwich. "What is this?"

"You don't like the cream cheese and cucumber?" Mom asked.

Maddie had just taken a bite of the same thing. She choked it down and then made a face that almost mirrored Mia's. "No, no, no!"

Miss Julia poured Maddie and Mia each a cup of steaming tea, using the strainer to catch the tea leaves so they wouldn't end up in the cups. "Why don't you wash that one down with this?"

"I bet you'll like the brie and pear, though." Mom pointed out another sandwich.

"You have to eat them with your pinkie up, like this," Dad said, holding his pinkie high.

Maddie took a bite, more carefully this time, relaxing as the sweet and creamy tastes filled her mouth. "Much better."

Mia added a lump of sugar, and then another, to her cup of tea.

"Try it, why don't you, before you keep adding sugar," Dad said.

Mia gave him her most innocent smile and then took a sip. "Delicious."

"I think tea is di-vine," Lulu said, reaching for a cookie.

"Not lov-e-ly?" Mia teased.

Lulu shot Mia a look and Maddie could see an argument about to start. She tried to think of something distracting to say, but all she could think of was telephone booths and frogs turning into princes.

"Lulu, try a sandwich," Mom said, handing one over. "Ham and cheese. You'll like it."

Lulu ate it in three bites. "Okay, fine, that was good. But not as good as chocolate!"

"What are these?" Mia asked, reaching for a square chocolate with a flower design on top.

"Those are petit fours," Miss Julia said, "which is a French name. In the 18th century the French made these teeny sweets in ovens."

"Don't say French too loud around here," Dad warned.

"Why not?" Mia asked, eyes wide.

"There's a very long rivalry between the two countries," Miss Julia said. "You'll hear about it on the Tower of London tour."

"What's a rivalry?" Lulu asked.

Maddie loved that Lulu always asked any question that popped into her mind. Either Maddie knew the answer, and then she felt smart because she could answer, or she didn't, and she was relieved not to have to be the one to ask.

"A rivalry is a sort of competition that has been going on for a very long time—one that might flare up at any moment," Mom said.

"Like how Mia and I sometimes fight about whose plan is the best one?" Lulu asked.

"You know, there is a thing called sibling rivalry," Dad said, "But most of the time, I think you girls avoid it. Not too much competition in this family. You've all carved out your own unique space for yourselves, I'd say."

Mia grinned and Lulu bounced on her seat, both delighting in the compliment, but Maddie twisted the corner of her napkin. She'd expected London to be all fun all the time, but somehow, things felt off-balance here too. Jangly. That was how she felt . . . or what was that word she'd learned recently? *Cacophony.* Maybe that was the word. Her insides felt noisy and chaotic, and it was hard to remember that no one else could hear.

"What do you think of the tea, Maddie?" Mom asked.

Maddie smoothed out her napkin. Enough. She was fine, and whatever cacophony thing was going on inside of her would eventually sort itself out. She was sure it would.

"You're right, Mom, the clotted cream is delicious," Maddie said.

Mom could always read Maddie's face. Probably, Mom could see more of the cacophony than Maddie realized, but still, she wouldn't push. Mom waited until Maddie was ready to talk and never put her on the spot in front of everyone.

"I want to have tea at the Savoy every day," Lulu announced, snatching the last petit four before anyone else could.

Mia leaned back in her seat. "I'm stuffed!"

"Me too," Miss Julia said. "But I'm stuffed in the best kind of way . . . Ready to take London by storm."

"Good thing too," Mom said, smiling. "You'll need all that energy later to keep up with these girls."

"True!" Miss Julia said.

"Shall we head back to our carriage before it turns into a pumpkin?" Dad asked, as he finished paying the bill.

"Our carriage? What pumpkin?" Lulu asked.

"Cinderella . . ." Mia said.

"OH!" Lulu said, standing up and twirling. "I get it now."

"Come on, my sweetest of princesses," Mom said, leading the way.

Maddie hoped she'd be swept up into the fun of it all again very soon.

SIX

Everyone wanted to walk after all of that food, so
they decided to take the sidewalk along the river. As
they waited at a crosswalk, a uniformed man rode by on
a horse. He wore a black helmet that tilted low over his
eyebrows, making his eyes look shadowed and stern.

"Who's that?" Lulu asked as the light changed and
they crossed the street. "Why's he riding a horse?"

"That," Mom said, "is a bobby. Actually, I have a
story for you about bobbies."

"What's a bobby?" Mia asked.

"That's what I'm going to tell you." Mom sat on a
bench and waited while everyone gathered around.
"Grandma's great-great-great grandfather"—Mom
ticked off greats on her fingers—"was named Sir Robert
Peel. He was called 'Sir' because he was knighted by
the queen. And do you want to know what he did?
He invented the London police force. He thought that
London needed officers to protect the people, so he
decided who should be an officer and what they should
wear. Now they call all the officers in London bobbies,
after Robert Peel. Even though his name was Robert,
everyone called him Bob. And that's why they started
calling the police bobbies."

"Whoa!" Lulu gasped.

43

"Awesome!" Maddie said, watching the bobby ride away.

"So we're royalty?" Mia asked.

Miss Julia, Mom, and Dad all burst out laughing.

"Not exactly," Mom finally said.

"But we're Glimmer girls!" Lulu jumped off the bench and started to dance around. "Let's say our family motto Mommy wrote for us!"

All the girls chorused, "Glimmer girls, sparkle and shine, but most of all, be kind."

As she chimed along, Maddie's gloominess began to fade. Even if she wasn't sure what her special place in the Glimmer family was yet, she knew that being a Glimmer girl was a good thing to be. Being a Glimmer girl meant she got to come to London and have tea at the Savoy and learn about bobbies and ride in strange cabs and pose for pictures on top of bronze lions. It meant she got to watch concerts in which her mom sang for thousands of people, and then bask in the glow she always felt when Mom sang the song she'd written especially for them. It meant she got to have Mia for a twin. Even when being a twin was hard, it was the best thing in the world to have a sister she could trust and have adventures with and even swap secrets with too. And being a Glimmer girl also meant Maddie got to have Lulu for a little sister—Lulu, who always made Maddie laugh and who helped her be brave enough to try things she wouldn't try otherwise.

"Wait a second!" Lulu said, throwing out her arms and catching both of her sisters in their stomachs.

"Ouch, Lulu!" Mia said.

"Oof!" Maddie said.

Lulu rounded on them with fingers in the air. "Our great-great-great . . . well, whatever . . . old guy in our family *invented* the police. That means we should be excellent at solving crime. Like the mystery of who stole my suitcase, for instance."

"No one stole your suitcase, Lulu," Mia said. "It was just lost along the way."

"You don't know that," Lulu said. "Anything could have happened to it."

"I'll bet they've delivered it to our hotel room already," Mia said.

"But what if they haven't? What if someone took it and—"

"And what? They're playing with your toys? Do you really think that would happen?" Mia asked.

Lulu started to sing a few notes that sounded like the beginning of a theme song. "The Glimmer girls are on the case!"

Maddie couldn't help laughing. At least Lulu wasn't crying over the suitcase anymore.

"It would be fun to be detectives, wouldn't it?" Maddie asked Mia.

"But what would we investigate?" Mia asked. "Who would the suspects be?"

"We can look for clues!" Lulu shouted, continuing on with her theme song.

Another bobby clopped past on his horse, and Lulu shouted after him, "We're related to Sir Robert Peel!"

"Is that right?" The bobby circled back and dismounted.

"Actually, it is," Mom said. "I was just telling the girls about their great-great-great grandfather, and about why London police are called bobbies."

"Fascinating," he said.

"So, we're going to investigate our first crime," Lulu said.

"Really, and what is that?" the bobby asked.

"Someone stole my suitcase," Lulu said.

"Actually, it got lost on our flight," Mia said.

Maddie looked from Mia to Lulu, praying her sisters wouldn't get in a fight right now, not in front of a police officer.

Instead of looking annoyed, though, the bobby nodded and pursed his lips. Then, after consideration, he said, "I suppose the suitcase could have been stolen. Or it could have been lost. When something goes wrong, the first thing a bobby must do is to think through all of the possibilities. We must never rule out any scenarios until we're sure they're impossible."

"What's the second thing a bobby does?" Lulu asked.

"Well, usually we'd look for obvious clues. Then, if it appears the situation truly is a crime, we'd call for backup. That's because three minds are always better than one."

"So we should look for clues!" Lulu bounced up and down on her toes. "About my suitcase!"

"You can certainly keep your eyes open," the bobby said. "Are the airline officials looking for your suitcase?"

"Yes," Mia said.

"Well, then, if it were me, first I'd see what they discover. If they can't find your suitcase in a reasonable amount of time, maybe it's time to dig a little deeper. In any case, it's good to have such clever minds on the case. Particularly minds that descended from Sir Robert Peel."

"What does descended mean?" Lulu asked.

"That means he's your relative from a long time ago," Mom said. "And now, Glimmer girls, I think it's time for us to say good-bye to our new friend."

"True. I should head out on my patrol," the bobby said, remounting his horse.

"Good-bye!" they all called and waved.

Mid-wave, Lulu let out a huge yawn. Maddie found herself yawning too.

"We're all tired," Mom said. "But every girl deserves to see the lights of London. Let's ride around a little and then we can go back to the hotel and get a great night's sleep."

"Sounds perfect," Dad said, wrapping an arm around her and raising his other hand to hail a new cab.

SEVEN

We're here!" Lulu announced, pushing her way through the concert hall doors.

She bolted down the aisle the way Mom always told her not to do, because she might stumble and fall into one of the seats. Lulu never fell though—the faster she went, the more sure-footed she seemed. Once Lulu made it to the stage, she hurried up the steps and threw herself into one band member after another's arms for giant hugs.

"We're in London!" she announced with each hug. "London!"

Maddie and Mia made it up to the stage after Lulu, but they also made the rounds, handing out hugs. Maddie loved every single person in Mom's band. And even though she knew they'd be there for the concert, it was always surprising seeing them in each city on tour—like running into your aunts and uncles halfway around the world.

"So, we think we should sing a song in Mom's concert," Mia said to Richie, the drummer.

"Your own song, huh?" he said, smiling over at Mom. "And what would you sing?"

"Something about dreaming big, I think," Mia said.

"I'll be the star!" Lulu said, leaping and twirling, nearly tripping over a coiled-up cord.

Dad caught her, laughing. "If there's a Glimmer girls song, all three of you will be the stars."

Lulu's face fell. Mia knew the song wasn't the only problem; there was also Lulu's dashed plans to be the Glimmer Girls Detective Agency. This morning, her suitcase arrived at the hotel just after Mom and Dad had left. Even though Lulu was happy to have her toys back, she'd really wanted to be a detective and figure out who stole her suitcase.

"It's okay, Lulu," Maddie said. "Maybe the Glimmer girls will find another case."

"I knew your suitcase wasn't stolen," Mia said, and then when Maddie shot her a *be-careful* look, she threw up her hands in innocence. "What?"

"The suitcase showed up?" Mom asked.

"Yes." Lulu looked more like a wilted tulip than her usual, radiant self.

"The airline delivered it this morning just after you left," Miss Julia said. "Apparently, they accidentally sent it to Paris rather than to London."

"Lulu, your suitcase visited the Eiffel Tower!" Mom said. "That's fantastic."

"I want to visit the Eiffel Tower!" Lulu wailed.

Clearly, the situation was going downhill.

"You know what, Lulu?" Mom said, "We may not have time to prep a song for you girls to sing with me while we're in London, but maybe you can sing with me in a concert another time. It might be a lot of fun, actually. We should try out a song with the band to see how it feels. Want to?"

"Right now?" Lulu's eyes went wide.

"Yes, yes, yes!" Mia said, pumping her fists.

Maddie's stomach twisted into a knot. Even though everyone in the room was a friend, she couldn't imagine singing, right here, right now. Maybe Mia and Lulu thought it would be fun to jump around and sing when they weren't ready, but to Maddie, that sounded like the most embarrassing thing in the world. Even when she'd prepared for weeks for her piano concerts, her hands still shook on her way to the stage.

"I think we should sing 'This Little Light of Mine.'" Mom turned to her band. "What do you all think? Can we rock out that old-school children's song, Glimmer girls' style?"

Richie beat out a rhythm in response. Everyone scurried to hook up instruments, pick up guitars, and adjust amps. Miss Julia and the three backup singers headed out to the theater seats. Dad handed Mia, Lulu, and Maddie wireless microphones.

"You can do this, Mads," Dad said. "Just sing like no one's watching."

The trouble was, everyone was watching.

Dad counted everyone in, and started the first chords on the piano. As the music started up, the drums, guitars, and piano all rumbled through Maddie's body, making her feel full and tingly and ready to dance. Mia and Lulu danced in time with the music.

"This little light of mine, I'm gonna let it shine," Mom started.

Mia and Lulu sang along. The sound filled the entire room, and Maddie could hear each distinct voice—Mom, Mia, Lulu. She stared at the microphone in her hands. Opening her own mouth to join in seemed impossible.

"Come on, Maddie," Mia called, bumping her with her hip. "Sing with us!"

With effort, Maddie opened her mouth and began singing along. At first, her voice sounded like a rusted old gate, squeaky and awkward. She was sure that as soon as anyone heard it, they'd laugh. But as the song continued, she realized everyone was smiling and having fun. No one was laughing at her. Mia caught her eye and grinned, nodding encouragement. Maddie let go inch by inch, and soon she was truly singing out loud—she could hear her own voice weaving together with the others. Truthfully, she had to admit that singing with her mom and sisters was fun. She couldn't keep her feet still, thanks to the way the drummer kept beating out the rhythm. The band played the familiar song in a funky way, with the keys and bass taking the lead, making the song feel more like a party than anything else. As the last round of the chorus wound down, they all moved to center stage and sang their hearts out. Then, Miss Julia and the backup singers jumped to their feet and clapped and whistled and yee-hawed. Mom pulled all the girls into a giant hug and then they all bowed and bowed again.

Laughing, Mom went down to the auditorium to talk to Miss Julia about the day.

Maddie took Mia's hand and squeezed it. "Thank you."

"For what?" Mia asked.

"For making me sing, even when I didn't want to. It was fun."

"So does that mean you want to sing in a concert?" Mia asked.

"I can't wait to sing in a concert!" Lulu announced.

"No way!" Maddie said, not even having to think about it. "Not me."

"You never know," Mia said. "You might change your mind."

"Girls, are you ready to go to the National Gallery?" Miss Julia asked. "We have until seven tonight—that's when the concert starts."

"And we'll sing with Mommy!" Lulu shouted.

"Not tonight, Lulu," Mom said. "But maybe some-time soon. We'll see."

It was finally time to go see the paintings. Maddie checked her bag one more time to make sure she had her sketchbook and pencils. Hopefully she would have time to sketch a few of the paintings. Lots of artists did this, sitting in galleries and learning from famous painters by drawing versions of their images. Sitting with sketchbook and pencils in hand, Maddie felt the exact opposite of how she felt when she walked onstage to perform. Instead of the spotlight being on her, her own eyes were the spotlights. When she was drawing, she could see people and places clearly, much more clearly than she saw when she hurried by on her way somewhere. Especially with people. She'd see something inside of them, something absolutely unique to them, something you could draw but not necessarily put into words. Maybe what she was seeing, actually, was their glimmer. Maddie twined her pencil from finger to finger, thinking.

"What do you say we ride on a double-decker bus to the gallery?" Miss Julia asked.

"Is that like a double-decker ice cream cone?" Lulu asked.

"Similar. It's a bus with two floors. We can ride on the top, which is a little like sitting on the roof," Miss Julia said.

"Seriously?" Mia asked.

"Seriously," Miss Julia said.

"See you soon, girls," Dad called from the piano.

"I hope you have a spectacular day." Mom gave Mia and Lulu hugs. When she pulled Maddie in tight, she whispered in her ear, "I'm proud of you."

Maddie hugged Mom back. Her sisters and Miss Julia were on their way out the door, so she ran to catch up.

"Bye!" they all called, and headed out of the hall for the day's adventure.

EIGHT

When they stepped outside, the wind whipped their hair every which way. Maddie was glad she'd worn her hair up in a ponytail, so at least it was out of her eyes.

Mia fought the wind to wrestle her jacket closed. "You said it would rain all the time, Miss Julia, but it hasn't rained at all since we've been here."

Miss Julia checked the sky. "We'll see what happens. I'm carrying my umbrella, just in case."

"Mommy says carrying an umbrella makes it so it *won't* rain," Lulu said.

"Well, her theory has turned out to be correct so far," Miss Julia said, trying to keep her big yellow hat on her head and finally giving up. She took it off and juggled that, the umbrella, and her purse in her arms, letting her frizzy, red hair fly wildly.

"Too bad you can't carry something to make the wind go away," Mia said.

"I like the wind," Lulu said, jumping up and holding out her arms. "Look, it can almost pick me up."

"Careful, or you might get blown out into the street," Miss Julia said.

Lulu frowned at Miss Julia. "But I'm a long way from the street."

"She's teasing you," Mia said, putting an arm around her little sister.

Lulu wrinkled her nose at Mia and then ducked away, turning her attention to hopscotching along the sidewalk, avoiding the cracks. She was so busy watching her feet that she nearly missed the bus station.

"Lulu," Mia called. "Come back!"

"Huh?" Lulu stopped and looked back, her face registering surprise that they were all so far behind.

Maddie laughed. "You were about to walk away into London and leave the rest of us behind."

Lulu tip-tapped her toes. "Wouldn't it be fun to have a giant hide-and-go-seek game in London, like I could go hide and you all could come find me?"

"You wouldn't think that was so fun when we couldn't find you," Miss Julia said.

Lulu tilted her head, thinking. "No, I guess not, at least not after a little while. But at first it would be fun. All on my own, on the streets of London, having an adventure . . . ."

Maddie shuddered. To her, being alone on the streets of London sounded the opposite of fun . . . terrifying, even.

The double-decker bus pulled up the curb, every bit as red as the telephone booths.

"To the roof!" Lulu said, leading everyone upstairs.

It was the strangest sensation, climbing stairs on a bus and coming out on top. Maddie felt the slightest bit dizzy as they made their way to some open seats near the front. Even though she was sitting on the inside aisle, she could see down to the street. Looking down on the tops of all the cars made for an odd perspective. As the bus engine roared to life and they started moving, the buildings began zooming past. Up here, she felt like she was on a cloud ship, sailing through a foreign landscape, with the buildings rising above her head and extending down, down, down. Now the gargoyles and stone faces seemed close enough to reach out and touch. All around her, people snapped photos, pointing this way and that, making her feel she should look here and there and everywhere. Miss Julia snapped photos too, but Maddie was sure most of the picture would be taken up with her wild, red hair, rather than whatever she was trying to photograph.

Mia pointed out a pigeon who had landed on the railing. "Look, he's along for the ride!"

Just then, one of Lulu's favorite songs started playing over the speakers. She jumped up and started to dance and sing along.

"Lulu," Mia said, glancing back at the rest of the bus. "I don't think . . ."

Across the top level of the bus, everyone turned to watch and clap along with the music. Lulu wasn't going to stop now with so many people egging her on. As she always did when she had a captive crowd, Lulu turned on her extra-special charm. She pranced up and down the aisle, singing specifically to one group and then to another.

"Aren't you going to stop her?" Mia said.

Miss Julia snapped a photo. "She's not bothering anyone."

"She's . . ." Mia said, and then she looked over at Maddie and shrugged.

The song rose to a crescendo, and Lulu's voice rose along with it all the way to the end. Then she dropped into a low curtsey and started blowing kisses at everyone.

"Tips, tips?" she called.

"And that's the end of that," Miss Julia said, jumping up and sweeping Lulu back to their seats.

"What?" Lulu asked. "What did I do?"

"You can't ask random people on the bus for tips, Lulu," Mia said, eyebrows raised in what she probably hoped was an *I'm serious* face.

Even so, Maddie could see a smile threatening to break through. Lulu got away with things by leaping into them so quickly that no one had time to stop her. And who knew? If Miss Julia hadn't pulled her back to her seat, someone might even have given her a tip. That was just the way things went with Lulu—all part of the fun of having her for a little sister.

Lulu climbed onto her seat, scooting close to Miss Julia. "How much longer?"

"We're almost there," Miss Julia answered. "I think we're just a few blocks away."

"What are you drawing, Maddie?" Lulu asked.

Maddie turned her sketchbook so Lulu could see. She'd drawn her little sister, arms stretched up to the London sky, her mouth open as she sang, and the other bus passengers clapping along.

"Can I have that one?" Lulu asked.

"I don't think she should pull out pictures from her sketchbook. Her drawings should all be together—a record of our trip," Mia said.

"Like a travelogue," Miss Julia said.

"I want one," Lulu said, and then grinned at Mia. "A sketchbook, I mean, not the picture."

"You want to draw?" Miss Julia asked.

Lulu bit her lip. "Well, no. I don't know. Maybe."

"If you want a sketchbook, we might be able to find you one at the National Gallery. But maybe your travelogue could be different than Maddie's. Yours could have photos with captions, for instance."

"Oh, yes, let's do that!" Lulu said.

"There's an app I've been thinking about using," Miss Julia said. "We could use it on my phone to take pictures and keep some notes about our trip."

For the next few minutes, Lulu and Miss Julia were busy with her phone, installing and trying out the app.

Mia scooted over close to Maddie to look at her drawing again. "I like the way you sketched the faces— loose, but you can still see their expressions. Well, actually, it's like you can see what they're feeling, if you know what I mean."

"Really?" Maddie asked, warmth spreading through her despite the wind. "That's exactly what I was going for."

"Do you think there will be any paintings that we like at the National Gallery? Won't all of them be old?"

"I love seeing old paintings. I'd like to try to draw some of them."

"But sometimes old paintings are weird, like in colors I wouldn't choose, or . . . well, sometimes, they're naked people."

"True," Maddie said. "I'm not sure why artists were always painting naked people."

Miss Julia looked up from her phone. "Artists have always been fascinated with the human form. It wasn't meant to be about the nakedness. They were trying to capture what the human form truly looked like, on canvas."

"Well, I prefer seeing what they truly look like with clothes on," Mia said. "Just sayin.'"

At this, Miss Julia burst out laughing. "You girls are the best."

The bus came to a stop, and over the speaker, the driver announced, "The National Gallery."

"This is our stop," Miss Julia said, herding Maddie and her sisters toward the stairs.

"Bye!" "Have a fun trip!" "Nice singing!" the other passengers called.

Once they were off the bus, Miss Julia snapped a photo of the waving passengers for her new travelogue.

"We're back at Trafalgar Square!" Mia said.

"Race you to the lions!" Lulu said, and took off running.

NINE

Maddie tried to be patient while Lulu insisted on Miss Julia taking more pictures of the girls riding lions, this time for the travelogue. Then Mia and Lulu tossed coins into the fountain and made wishes.

"Why don't you make a wish?" Mia asked.

Maddie shifted from foot to foot. "Can't we please go into the gallery now? Please??"

"I think it's time, ladies," Miss Julia said. "Let's see what kinds of adventures the National Gallery has to offer."

"Last one there's a rotten egg!" Lulu shouted.

Miss Julia caught her mid-step. "Lulu, we need to talk about your running off. I know you're excited, but we're in a strange city and we're halfway around the world from home. In fact, even if we were at home, it would be important for us to all stay together."

"But if we're all racing, we'll be together," Lulu said. "Come on, please, please, please, can't we just race to the steps?"

"She can't outrun me," Mia said.

"Can too!"

"Can not!"

"Wanna bet?"

"Girls!" Miss Julia said. "All right. I'll count you off and you can race to the steps, but then you have to stop and we'll all go together. And no plowing into tourists, okay?"

"Okay!" Mia said. "Maddie, are you going to race too?"

Maddie looked down at her bag with sketchbook and pencils—not exactly convenient for racing. "Not this time."

"Okay, girls," Miss Julia said. "Ready, set, go!"

Mia and Lulu stayed neck and neck all the way across the square, but then at the last minute, Mia fell a few steps behind. Maddie was pretty sure she'd done it on purpose—sometimes Mia did the just-right thing.

"I won!" Lulu gasped, smiling ear to ear.

"Thank you," Maddie whispered to Mia.

"Today's going to be the best day ever," Mia whispered back, and then shouted so the world could hear, "Today's going to be the best day ever!"

A few tourists turned and smiled at this. One even snapped their picture.

"They're going to put that in their travel album with the caption: Crazy girls!" Maddie said.

The girls giggled their way up the huge stone steps. Inside, the National Gallery was just as impressive as it looked from the outside. They didn't have to pay, but they did have to walk through a metal detector before stepping into the echoing lobby. Steps led from the wide-open lobby to the second floor.

Miss Julia circled the information kiosk. "There's a special concert later today . . . Oh, but it's about the time we'll need to leave for your mom's concert."

"What kind of concert?" Lulu asked.

"It's a small orchestra—it seems they play every Friday and Saturday night." She studied a museum map. "Looks like most of the paintings are upstairs. Oh, and there are a few audio tours. Would you girls like an audio guide while we explore the museum?"

"Let me see!" Lulu said, pulling on the map to see the list.

"Art Detectives," Mia read over Lulu's shoulder. "That one sounds fun."

"Whoa, really?" Lulu asked, and then she spotted the title for herself. "Yes! The Glimmer girls have a new case!"

Maddie had to admit, it sounded fun to be an art detective, but what she really wanted was time to look at the art. Maybe the detective tour would help keep Lulu interested. If so, Maddie would have more time— hopefully enough to sketch too.

Miss Julia rented audio tour headsets, and they all listened to the introduction. The audio tour told the story of two special agents uncovering clues about the meanings of some of the most mysterious paintings in the collection. Maddie, Mia, Lulu, and Miss Julia climbed the marble stairs and then followed the tour from painting to painting. While Lulu looked for clues in each painting, Maddie sketched what she saw. The questions in the tour were actually pretty interesting. Maddie liked thinking about why a painter might have painted a specific image, or what the painting might have meant to him or her.

They wandered from room to room, each one painted a different color. Most of the rooms had about thirty paintings on the walls, even though the rooms were large enough to hold many more. Maddie liked the way each painting had its own space with lots of wall around it. She thought about what Dad had said at tea—that she and her sisters each had their own space in the Glimmer family. If she and her sisters were each paintings, Lulu would be bright colors—fireworks, maybe. Mia would be leading a charge, maybe not in a battle, but her painting would definitely be bold and brave. Maddie wasn't sure what kind of painting she'd be. Maybe she'd be one of the calm landscapes with trees and lakes and mountains.

"Come on, come on!" Lulu crowed, tugging on Maddie's arm.

Soon, they were in Room 43 with the Impressionist paintings. Maddie thought the Gallery should call the rooms by their colors. If they did, Room 43 would be the Purple Room, which sounded much nicer to Maddie. As she glanced around the walls, one of the paintings caught her eye.

"Look at this one!" She moved in closer to study the image.

"I like the colors—the blues, purples, and pinks," Mia said, joining her. "And it has just the right amount of detail."

Maddie tilted her head one way and then the other. "I like the way the paint is so textured, with all the mixing in the clouds and the water and the rocks."

Miss Julia came over and stood next to Maddie, reading the plaque. "It's called *Moulin Huet Bay, Gurnsey*. It's by Renoir."

"I don't think that's the right name for this painting at all," Maddie said. "It should be called something like . . ."

"Beachside Blues!" Lulu suggested.

"Maybe . . ." Maddie said. "But when you have the blues, you're sad. In the painting, the people are playing in the ocean and having a lot of fun."

"So what would you call it?" Mia asked.

"Something that describes the way the paint is done in all of those splotches, like, I don't know . . . maybe 'Sun-Splattered Afternoon.'"

"I like that," Mia said. "Like *Starry Night*. A painting's name should describe what the painting is all about."

"Too bad Renoir isn't here so you could suggest that to him," Miss Julia said. "What else do you like about the painting, Maddie?"

"Well . . ." Maddie started.

"What's that?" Lulu asked, loud enough to stop everyone in the room.

"Hush, Lulu," Mia said.

"No really, what is that?" Lulu pointed to the oddest painting in the room. It was a face, or something like a face, but everything was in the wrong place.

"Lulu, you're being rude," Mia said, pulling her away from the painting.

"Stop pulling me."

"Well, stop shouting. You're making everyone look."

It was true. Everyone in the room was looking. In fact, a security guard had started toward them, probably to tell Lulu it wasn't appropriate to shout in a museum.

"You know what, girls," Miss Julia said, redirecting them toward the gallery door. "Maybe it's time for lunch. There's a dining room here at the Gallery that has excellent reviews."

"But no one has answered my question," Lulu said. "Why is everything in the wrong place on that painting? Why would a painter do that?"

"We can talk about it later," Mia said.

It had to be a pretty embarrassing moment to make Mia turn bright red, and her cheeks were flaming. Maddie would have been embarrassed too, if she weren't so frustrated. She'd really wanted to look at "Sun-Splattered Afternoon" and to answer Miss Julia's question. Sometimes in this family there wasn't time to think. Every time she started to think about something for real, someone interrupted and they were off again in some new direction, leaving Maddie and her thoughts behind.

Miss Julia and her sisters were nearly out of the gallery. Maddie had to jog to catch up, glancing back one more time at the painting. Her head filled with the words she would have liked to say to Miss Julia about what she liked about the paint and the figures and the artist's style. Renoir's style.

"When we come back, can we still be art detectives?" Lulu asked.

"We can," Miss Julia said, leading the way downstairs to the dining room.

Maddie had to admit her stomach was growling. Maybe she could bargain for another look at "Sun-Splattered Afternoon" after lunch.

TEN

In the National Gallery Restaurant, the waiter gave them their choice of seats, because the restaurant hadn't filled up yet for lunch. They chose a table near the windows where they could look out over Trafalgar Square.

After looking over the menu, they chose Shirley Temples with cherries on top to drink, a couple orders of fish and chips to share, and a salad, which they all promised to eat a few bites of—even Lulu.

As Miss Julia took out an activity book for Lulu, Mia slid over close to Maddie.

"What's the matter?" Mia asked.

"What do you mean?"

"You're so quiet. You've barely said three words since we sat down to eat."

Maddie shrugged. "I'm okay."

"Come on, Maddie. I know you. You're obviously not okay. What's wrong?"

Maddie glanced over at Lulu, but her little sister and Miss Julia were too busy with the activity book to listen to their conversation.

"I was in the middle of talking with Miss Julia about that painting—you know, 'Sun-Splattered Afternoon,' and then Lulu made all that commotion and we had to leave."

"Did you really like the paintings, though?" Mia asked. "I mean, most of them were . . . I don't know . . . old, don't you think?"

"Well, yes, they're old, but isn't that what people like about them?"

"Is that what you like about them?"

"No. I don't know. It's interesting that they're old. I like thinking about the painters who lived a long time ago and painted them."

"Would you want to hang one of them in our house? I mean, if we could actually do that?"

"Not most of them, no. But maybe 'Sun-Splattered Afternoon.' I liked the colors and the texture of the paint. If you looked at the painting one way, it was just a bunch of splotches, but together they made such a beautiful picture of the sand and the sea. You know how when you're at the beach and there's sand and salt water and wind, and the air feels thick, like it has texture . . . Do you know what I mean? That's what the painting made me think of—the way the air feels at the beach. I wanted more time to look at it, maybe even time to sketch it."

"Lulu's always interrupting, Maddie. You should be used to it by now," Mia said.

"It's not her fault. I know I shouldn't be upset. I'm fine."

"You're not," Mia said. "Just because Lulu is younger doesn't mean she should always get her way."

"I don't want to fight about it," Maddie said.

"You never want to fight," Mia said. "But then you don't stand up for yourself and you end up not getting to do the things you really want to do."

"But I don't actually *need* to look at that painting," Maddie said.

"I know that, but you want to. We should go back and look at it."

Before Maddie could stop her, Mia turned to Miss Julia. "We're looking at more paintings after lunch, right?"

"We certainly have more paintings to see," Miss Julia said.

"And we haven't finished solving the art detective mystery," Lulu said.

"Could we go back to Maddie's painting?" Mia asked. "The one she was just looking at?"

"Well, of course," Miss Julia said.

"Do we have to?" Lulu asked. "We've already seen that one. I want to solve the mystery!"

"How about we finish solving the mystery, and then go see Maddie's painting as our final treat of the day?" Miss Julia suggested.

"Deal!" Lulu banged her fists on the table, making all of the silverware jump with a clatter. "Oops!"

Maddie and Mia started to giggle. Lulu held out, but not for long. Soon, tears filled Maddie's eyes and her stomach started to burn, but every time she managed to stop laughing someone would snort or squeal and she'd burst out laughing all over again.

When the waiter showed up with their food, they finally managed to get themselves under control. He placed fancy plates in front of each of them with a flourish. Maddie nearly started giggling again over the odd combination of french fries and fish on such fancy china, all placed carefully on a white tablecloth-covered table.

"May I bring you anything else?" the waiter asked.

"I think we're all set," Miss Julia said.

"Cheers!" he answered, leaving them to eat.

"Why is everyone always saying 'Cheers' around here?" Lulu asked, reaching for one of her french fries—chips, as they called them in London. "What does that word mean, exactly?"

"Cheers can mean a lot of things," Miss Julia said. "Thank you, or good wishes, or even hello, depending on who's saying it and when."

"Then why don't they actually say thank you or hello?" Lulu asked.

"Because saying cheers is so much cooler," Mia said, and then tried out the word with an English accent. "Cheers!"

"God bless this meal," Miss Julia said. "And make us a blessing to the people around us today."

"Amen," chimed the girls, and then everyone dug in.

It turned out that fried fish was much more delicious than most other kinds of fish. And the french fries were perfectly crispy too. Apparently, you were supposed to eat them with vinegar, like salt and vinegar potato chips. Maddie chose good-old-American ketchup, which she was relieved to find on the table alongside the vinegar.

"It's good, Maddie," Mia insisted, holding a vinegar-soaked fry out in front of Maddie's face. The smell made the inside of Maddie's nose burn.

"No, thanks," Maddie said.

"Suit yourself," Mia said, and popped the whole fry in her mouth. "Mmmm . . ."

Soon, every last chip had been inhaled. The fish wasn't quite as popular, but between the four of them, they nearly finished the lot. And Lulu's bites of salad were miniature, but in the end, she did swallow them down.

"So, are we ready to solve our mystery?" Miss Julia asked.

"And see Maddie's 'Sun-Splattered Afternoon'!" Mia reminded everyone.

"Let's go!" Lulu jumped to her feet and nearly toppled a water glass in the process.

"Oops-a-daisy," the waiter said, catching the glass just in time.

"Wow! Nice catch," Mia said.

As they stood to go, the waiter stepped aside to let them pass. "Cheers!"

"Why do you say cheers instead of thank you?" Lulu asked. "Do you ever say plain thank you?"

"Well now . . . ." the waiter said, thinking. "I definitely do say thank you every now and again, but cheers is my go-to, I suppose."

"Thank you for all of your help today," Miss Julia said.

"Yes," Lulu said, and then in her best English accent, "Cheers!"

The waiter gave them a broad smile. "Now you sound like a right little English maiden. The best to all of you in your travels."

"The Glimmer girls are on the case!" Lulu said, and then launched into her theme song again.

"Shhh, Lulu," Mia warned.

Maddie just smiled. Lulu made everything more fun, theme songs and all.

ELEVEN

They had three more rooms to visit on the Art Detective tour. In Room 9, the room Maddie would call the green room, all the paintings were from Venice. They were also huge. The painting on the Art Detectives tour was called *Christ Addressing a Kneeling Woman*. The woman knelt in front, with a crowd pressing in around her and Christ standing next to her. Like many of the paintings with Jesus in them, he had a white glow around his head to show his holiness.

"His eyes are so kind," Mia said. "I like to think of Jesus looking like that. Wouldn't it be amazing if we actually had lived in those times and could have looked at him? I mean, to look at God? He wouldn't have had that glow. If you passed him on the street, I wonder if you'd know he wasn't an ordinary person."

"I think if you talked to him, you'd have known," Maddie said. "In all the Bible stories, even when Jesus wasn't preaching, he said the kinds of things that surprised people and made them think."

"What are we supposed to figure out in this painting?" Lulu asked.

They listened to the audio, and then tried to figure out what the other people in the painting were thinking, each person a little different than the others.

On their way out of the room, Maddie stopped to look at a painting called *Mary Magdalene*. The colors were muted—grays and browns and blues. Mary Magdalene sat curled up, her shawl wrapped around her shoulders and knees. She seemed to be thinking deeply. Maybe if she could be a painting, Maddie would want to be one like this. Even though it wasn't fireworks or a courageous charge, this painting made you stop to think.

They finished up the Art Detective tour, and Lulu gave one final rendition of the Glimmer girls theme song. Fortunately, the last stop of the tour was in the children's hall, so no one really minded.

Maddie hurried from the children's hall up the stairs to the purple room, only just keeping herself from running, something she knew she should never do in a museum. It was finally time to see "Sun-Splattered Afternoon" again, and this time, she would have as much time as she wanted to look at it.

"Hold up," Mia called, jogging to catch up.

"Wait for me!" Lulu said, her high voice approaching the kind of wail that Maddie knew would turn to tears if she wasn't careful.

She slowed down and waited for Lulu and Miss Julia to catch up. Then, together, they made their way through one room after another. It was odd, the way that nearly no one was in any of the rooms right then.

"I think it's so quiet because everyone is gathered downstairs for that special concert," Miss Julia said, flagging down a nearby guard to ask him if that was the case.

When they were about to step into the Purple Room, Maddie saw a gloved man reach up and take a painting off the wall. She pulled her sisters back behind a pillar and peeked around to see what he was doing. People weren't supposed to take paintings off the wall, Maddie was absolutely sure of that. This man glanced over his shoulder, as if to check to make sure he was alone, and then he hurried away into the next room.

Maddie stood frozen, completely unsure of what to do.

"Did you see that?" Mia asked, eyes as round as saucers.

"He—" Lulu began in her voice that carried across any room, but Mia clapped her hand over their little sister's mouth.

"Shhh!"

"Yeah," Maddie said, and then realized she knew exactly what they should do. "Come on!"

She raced after the man, who seemed to have disappeared into thin air in the next room. A door clicked, and she knew he'd gone into an employees-only area.

"Should we follow him?" she asked Mia.

"I don't know . . ." Mia said. "Maybe he's an employee and we just misunderstood."

"But did you see the way he looked over his shoulder, like he was doing something wrong? People who work here wouldn't do something like that. Plus, why would he be taking a painting off a wall all by himself?"

"He's getting away!" Lulu wailed.

"Maybe we can cut him off somewhere," Mia said. "Maybe he'll come out of the employee door downstairs."

"What's going on, girls?" Miss Julia asked, catching up with them. "You can't just go running off like that."

Maybe Mia was the one who'd usually lead a charge, but Maddie wasn't going to let this criminal get away. Not only had she been waiting all day to see "Sun-Splattered Afternoon," but it was wrong to take a painting, something that had been made so long ago and which could never be replaced.

Maddie made up her mind. Even if it was against the rules to run in a museum, this situation was obviously the exception. "He's getting away!" she called to her sisters.

TWELVE

Maddie sprinted for the stairs, hoping Mia was right about him coming out an employee door downstairs. It didn't seem like the man would want to come out into the main hall with a painting under his arm, but he wouldn't want to stay in the employee area either. Not if he was stealing the painting. Anyone could see him.

"Maddie, where are you going?" Miss Julia called after her.

Maddie glanced over her shoulder. Once again they were like a parade. Mia, then Lulu, with Miss Julia hurrying along after them, trying to keep her cool as she passed a guard.

"Hey!" he called, and started after them. "You can't run in here."

Maddie took the stairs two at a time, hoping she wouldn't fall flat on her face. No time to worry about that now. All that mattered was finding the thief before it was too late.

Maddie put on a burst of speed down the last two stairs and rounded the corner. *Crash!* She skidded to a stop, and Mia thumped into her back, causing another loud crash. Blinking, Maddie realized they'd run straight into a cellist, knocking her cello out of her hands. *Crash!*

Lulu plowed into a whole section of music stands and scattered them. Sheet music flew everywhere.

"Oh no, no, no!" The cellist knelt beside her fallen cello, running her fingers over the sides of the instrument, inspecting every last inch.

Maddie stood helplessly, remembering what Mom always said about orchestra instruments in particular. *They're expensive, girls, very expensive. Whatever you do, you must be careful if there are instruments involved.* Of all the things she could have run into, why did it have to be a cello?

"What were you thinking?" The cellist's voice felt as sharp as a slap.

Maddie stared at her toes, not able to meet the cellist's eyes.

"Now there." A violinist tucked her instrument under her arm and knelt next to the cellist to take a look. "I don't see any damage."

"So, your cello is okay?" Maddie asked, praying this was the truth.

"No thanks to you," the woman snapped. "And I think there's a scratch. I'm not sure."

Mia hurried to pick up the music stands and Lulu tried to help.

"Leave them," the conductor said.

By now, most of the instrumentalists had gathered round, wearing grim expressions. A few murmured soothing words to the cellist.

"We're so sorry," Maddie said, tears filling her eyes.

"Don't think you can cry about this and get away with it," the cellist said. "You'll pay if there's anything wrong with my cello."

"She didn't mean . . ." Miss Julia began, trying to sooth the angry woman.

The security guard spoke into her radio urgently, and then clapped a hand on Maddie's shoulder. "I think you should all come with me."

Maddie's stomach dropped. For a moment, she couldn't move.

Mia slipped her hand into Maddie's and whispered in her ear, "It's okay. Don't worry."

"But what about my cello?" the cellist asked no one in particular.

"Bring your cello along. If need be, we will certainly work out a way for you to file a claim. You say there's no damage you can see?" The security guard frowned down at the cello.

"Well, no," the cellist admitted, placing her cello back in its case. "But I won't know if my instrument is ruined until I truly play it. Anything could have happened to the balance, tiny things, things the naked eye could never see."

"Well, then, you can exchange information. Come with me, and we'll get this handled," the security guard said.

The thief! Maddie suddenly remembered why they'd been running in the first place. "But we can't leave. We have to find the thief!"

"The what?" the security guard asked, reaching for her radio again.

"A man took a painting off a wall upstairs. We were running to catch up with him. What if we made it easier for him to get away because we made this giant mess?"

"If there had been a robbery, I'm sure I'd know about it," the security guard said, checking her radio's knobs and dials.

"But—" Maddie said.

"Girls, let's go." Miss Julia looked more serious than Maddie had ever seen her look.

They followed the guard through another employees-only door, and up a cement staircase to the second floor. Behind them, the cellist followed, carrying her cello even though the case was huge and looked nearly impossible to lug up the stairs. A security door opened into a reception area. Behind the wide desk, a number of offices lined a long hallway.

"Wait here," the guard said, indicating a couch and chairs.

"Would you like something to drink?" the woman behind the desk asked. "Tea or water?"

"Oh, no . . ." Miss Julia said, looking embarrassed as the guard shot them a withering glance. "But thank you."

"I'll take tea," the cellist piped up.

The receptionist looked from the girls to the musician and back again, but didn't comment as she rose to pour tea into a mug. "Milk or sugar?"

The cellist sniffed. "Both."

The receptionist gave the girls an apologetic look as she handed off the tea. Lulu begged to take a picture for the travelogue, while Miss Julia tried to explain the seriousness of the situation. Mia tossed in a comment now and again, but Maddie couldn't focus on the conversation. If she were a painting now, she'd be a messy black storm. A woman came out of one of the offices talking on her phone.

"It should be ready in a day or two," the woman said, and then nodded to the receptionist.

Maddie noticed that the woman had paint under her fingernails, the way her art teacher always did. It made sense that artists would work at museums, but she thought it might be difficult too. Wouldn't it be hard to be around art all the time and not be able to paint yourself?

"Yes, the Renoir," the woman said as she passed through the door.

Maddie frowned. The stolen painting had been a Renoir, and now this woman had mentioned one. Did that mean the museum had discovered the robbery? She stood up, meaning to stop the woman and tell her they'd seen the thief, but just then the security guard showed up.

"The director can see you now." She motioned them toward one of the offices.

Maddie didn't think she should argue, not with the cellist, Miss Julia, Mia, and the security guard all giving her their most serious you're-in-trouble-now faces. She'd have to wait and tell the director about the thief. If one of the staff knew about the robbery, surely the director did too.

THIRTEEN

The director's office was very much like a principal's office, with floor to ceiling bookshelves, and a no-nonsense desk behind which the director sat. He motioned to the seats across from him, and steepled his fingers on his desk as he eyed the girls one by one. Maddie had never been to the principal's office because she was in trouble, but she had been there once with Mia and Mom to talk about class placement—whether the twins should be in the same classroom or each in their own. Even though that conversation had been important, she hadn't felt scared or guilty, the way she felt now. In fact, she couldn't remember ever having felt this badly before. She'd never, ever want to knock over an instrument on purpose. Even more importantly, she'd failed at stopping the thief, and all the commotion they'd made may have even made it easier for him to escape. Instead of helping, she'd made a giant mess.

"Now what's this I hear about running in the museum?" the director asked, after they'd all taken a seat.

"We saw a man steal a painting and . . ." Maddie started, thinking the director would be grateful for more information on the robbery.

"We don't know if he was stealing," Mia corrected.

The director smiled the smile that adults wore when they were trying to be patient, but weren't feeling very patient at all. "Girls, I don't have time for stories. The point is that you were running—"

"And you knocked over my cello!" the cellist roared. "That's what this is all about."

"Now, I'm sure the girls are sorry they knocked over your cello," the director jumped in, looking slightly alarmed at the volume of the woman's outburst. "And I'm sure they've learned their lesson, haven't you, girls?"

Maddie couldn't quite catch up with the conversation. Didn't the director know about the robbery? Had she totally misunderstood the conversation the woman was having on her phone?

"But we—" Maddie started.

"Maddie," Mia said, giving her a *stop-talking-now* look.

"Girls, don't you think you owe everyone an apology?" Miss Julia said.

"We're sorry," Lulu said. "But we were—"

"No buts," Miss Julia said.

"What will you do about my cello?" the cellist demanded.

"I understand you're upset," the director said. "But if your instrument is unharmed—"

"As I've been trying to tell you, we won't know whether it is harmed until the instrument is played, and not just a note or two, but when the instrument is truly warmed up and being used as it's meant to be used. Then I'll know if there are any damages."

"Someone stole a Renoir!" Maddie blurted. "We saw him take it right off the wall."

Everyone stopped and stared. Even Miss Julia looked a little shocked.

"You may have thought you saw . . ." the director began.

"I don't have time to sit here while these children make excuses for themselves," the cellist said. "My concert is in five minutes and I need to warm up my cello."

"Perhaps I can take your contact information?" the director asked Miss Julia. "Just in case?"

"Of course," Miss Julia said. She jotted a few lines on the director's notepad and passed it back to him.

"Thank you." The director stood and ushered the cellist toward the door. "Feel free to reach out if you need anything, and I'll be happy to connect you with Miss Julia and the girls. And now, I believe it's almost time for that concert of yours. I think I'll come down to hear you play."

"But what about the robbery?" Maddie asked.

The director waited until the cellist was out of the office and then gave Maddie his not-so-patient smile. "If there was a robbery in this museum, you can rest assured I'd be the first to hear about it."

"But—"

The director talked right over Maddie. "And if you think you see a crime, the best thing to do is to tell a security guard or a bobby about it. What if he'd been a real thief? What would you have done if you'd caught him?" the director asked.

"Pinned him to the ground and called for help!" Lulu announced.

Miss Julia shot her a warning look. "We'll be more careful in the future, won't we, girls?"

"Yes," they each said in turn.

The word felt bitter in Maddie's mouth. It wasn't fair that no one was listening to her when she'd only been trying to help. She shouldn't have been running—she knew that—but if she'd caught the thief, no one would be worried about the running, would they? They'd just be grateful she'd stopped the robbery. And of all the paintings, it had to be "Sun-Splattered Afternoon." It was such a beautiful painting, one that stood out from all the rest. Now it might be lost forever. The thought made her stomach twist up in knots all over again.

"It's time to go, girls. We should let the director get to the concert," Miss Julia said. "Thank you again for your help, sir."

"Anytime," he said. "It looks to me like the girls have learned their lesson."

"We have," Mia said, and elbowed Maddie.

Maddie nodded but didn't say anything. She knew the moment she opened her mouth, she'd start explaining herself all over again. No matter how much she said, it was clear no one would listen to her about the thief. If she wanted to stop him, it appeared she was on her own.

FOURTEEN

Just as they reentered the main hall, the conductor clicked his baton against the music stand, and the musicians all played a few notes to ensure they were in tune. Maddie listened for the cello—would it be off-key?

"Cello sounds fine to me," Mia said.

"I hope it is," Maddie said. "I feel awful about knocking it over. I never would have done that on purpose."

"In my opinion, she kind of overreacted," Mia said. "She could have been a little more understanding."

"I don't understand why no one knows about the painting yet. I mean, there's a gap on the wall where it used to hang. Anyone walking by would see that it's missing, wouldn't they?" Maddie asked.

Miss Julia guided them through the crowd and toward the front doors, away from the concert.

Mia's face lit up. "I know! We should go look for ourselves. Maybe the man wasn't a thief at all. If the painting is back on the wall, we wouldn't have to worry."

"Do you think we could?" Maddie asked.

"Miss Julia, can we go upstairs and look at Maddie's painting before we go?"

Miss Julia checked her watch. "With all of this running around, it's already six o'clock. Your mom's concert is in an hour. We need to get you back to the hotel and change clothes. And we need to eat dinner. I'm sure we'll be late as it is."

"Please, can't we just go look? Quickly?" Mia asked. "Maddie is really worried."

Miss Julia looked as though she was considering allowing them, but then she shook her head. "Girls, like the director said, this isn't your problem to solve. If a painting is truly missing, we need to let the museum deal with the situation. Anyway, I'm pretty sure there are alarms and other ways for the staff to know if a painting goes missing. You must have misunderstood what you saw."

Mia put an arm around Maddie and gave her a quick squeeze. "I'm sorry, Maddie. I tried."

"Can I have a bologna sandwich for dinner?" Lulu asked, bouncing up and down on her toes.

"We'll see what's on the room service menu," Miss Julia said.

Maddie dragged her feet the whole way out of the museum. Down the steps they went, and out into the wind-blown square. Flags snapped overhead.

A swift blast of wind caught Miss Julia's hat and blew it halfway into the square. They chased after it as it skittered along just out of reach.

"Wow, this wind!" Miss Julia said, after she'd jammed the hat back onto her head.

"Come on, Maddie, don't be upset." Mia gave Maddie another concerned look. "The cello will be fine."

Maddie opened her mouth to argue that the cello wasn't the point, the painting was, when something caught her eye. Rather, someone.

She squinted, her heartbeat speeding up. "I think . . ."

"What?" Mia asked.

"The thief! He was wearing a brown jacket with elbow patches, and he had gray streaks in his hair near his ears. And he wore glasses, the kind with the thin rims, right?"

"Yes . . ." Mia said.

"Well, I think that's him!" Maddie said, pointing. "And he has a package under his arm. A package the size of a painting. Look, Mia!"

Mia stood on her tiptoes, trying to see over people's heads. "I don't see him."

"Over there, just past the lion, leaving the square." Maddie was practically shouting now, willing Mia to see what she was seeing.

"I don't—" Mia began.

Maddie took off running, not waiting to hear the rest.

"Maddie Glimmer!" Miss Julia shouted, using the kind of voice that makes a person stop in her tracks.

Maddie stopped, but only after battling with herself about whether she should. She'd lost sight of the man. And even if she did spot him, like the director said, what would she do if she caught him, anyway?

Miss Julia took Maddie's hand with a firm grip. "Maddie, you know better than to run off. You all do. I realize you're excited, but I need for you—all of you—to make better choices."

"Did I make good choices today?" Lulu asked.

"Mostly," Miss Julia said, raising a stern eyebrow before relenting and breaking into a smile.

"If there had been a thief, I bet we could have caught him," Lulu said. "Remember how fast I ran across the square today?"

"Fast or slow, there will be no more running today," Miss Julia said. "We've had our fair share of running."

"Do you think the cellist will make the director call Mom?" Mia's voice was laced with worry.

"I think after she cools down, and especially if it turns out that her cello is okay, she'll let it go."

"Her cello sounded fine to me," Mia said.

"To me too," Miss Julia answered. "It's not doing us any good to worry."

"I don't think we should worry about the painting, either," Mia said. "I mean, don't you think the museum director would know if a painting vanished off the wall?"

"But I just saw the thief walking away with a painting," Maddie insisted.

"We don't know he's a thief," Mia said.

"We saw him," Maddie said. "You know we did."

"I'm just saying we shouldn't worry. Miss Julia is right. Nothing seems to be wrong at the museum."

"Everything is wrong." Tears pricked at the corners of Maddie's eyes.

"You know what?" Miss Julia said. "I think we need a breather. Let's hail a cab and get some dinner into all of those hungry stomachs. And try not to be any later for the concert than we already are, okay?"

"Okay," Mia said.

"We're sorry, Miss Julia," Lulu said, taking Miss Julia's hand.

Maddie couldn't bring herself to say anything at all, not during the walk or the cab ride, not while they put on their concert dresses, not even while they ate dinner—her favorite, mac and cheese.

Miss Julia snapped a couple pictures of their concert outfits for the travelogue. Then they were off again, on their way to the concert hall.

FIFTEEN

"Now, go in quietly, girls," Miss Julia warned, holding the door open.

Of course, at that moment, Mom had just walked up to the microphone to start a new song. The crowd had fallen silent.

Into the silence, Lulu shouted, "Hi, Mommy!"

Mom looked over at the girls—actually, everyone in the entire hall looked their way. Maddie cringed, feeling all those eyes focusing in on them. Behind her, she felt Miss Julia tensing up too.

"Glad you could join us," Mom said, smiling wide.

Maddie let out the breath she was holding and smiled back.

"Come on up here to your spot, girls," Mom said, waving them to the front.

Lulu led the way, waving to the crowd as she went. Maddie stuck close to Mia, relieved to have her sister right there by her side. Sometimes, Maddie wondered how Mom could stand it, being up on stage with all those people—strangers, most of them—watching her perform for hours. Maddie occasionally liked putting on a costume and acting, but that was different. That wasn't being yourself up on stage. When Maddie had to play concert recitals, her hands would shake like leaves in a windstorm while she sat in the audience waiting for her turn. Each time she'd be convinced she'd never be able to play. In the end, she'd calm down as soon as she put her fingers on the keys. But the walk up to the stage, out there in front of everyone, was very, very hard for her. This walk down the aisle wasn't quite so bad. Soon, they were in their usual spot, up close to the stage where they could almost reach out and touch Mom.

Mom nodded at Dad, who began to play, and the rest of the band joined in. "We're not here for me," Mom said, and then pointed to her band, "We're not here for them, either. We're here to give glory to God."

Maddie closed her eyes as Mom began to sing, letting the music and the words wrap around her, warm and soft and secure. She felt a tug on her arm.

"Maddie, someone over there is crying," Lulu whispered.

Maddie looked over and saw it was true. In fact, a couple people were blinking away tears. One woman, though, had tears streaming down her face.

"Do you think she's okay?" Lulu asked.

Mia put an arm around Lulu and said, "Mom always has such a way of reaching people with her music."

Lulu shook her head. "But I don't like it when they cry."

"Those aren't sad tears," Maddie said. "Remember when Mom cried when she sang us our song for the first time, when she was tucking us into bed? Hearing that song and watching her made me cry a little too."

The song rose to its climax, and then Mom sang a few more pieces. Finally, it was time for "When I Leave the Room," the song Mom had written just for them.

"I wrote this song for my little girls," Mom said. "It talks about all the wonderful, difficult, sorrowful parts of life, how God gives us people to hold and say I love you to, and people who say it back to us."

By the time the final notes played, Maddie's eyes had filled with tears, the way they always did when Mom sang this song. It didn't matter how many times Maddie heard it. She blinked hard and fast.

"Now, girls," Mom said, "it's time for you to go to the hotel, put on your pjs, and brush your teeth. I have just a few more songs to sing, but I'll see you in time to tuck you in."

This was the way it happened every time they came to listen. Maddie loved the tradition of it, the way she could count on Mom to say just these words the exact moment Lulu's eyes started to droop. Now, they'd go home and curl up under the covers of the big bed that she and Mia were sharing and read, and talk with Miss Julia about their day. Soon, Mom and Dad would be home. Everyone would pile into the same bed and Dad would tell them a story. She could tell her parents about what had happened, about the thief, and about what she suspected. They would help her know what she should do, and then, maybe everything that had gone wrong today would finally be okay.

SIXTEEN

Maddie snuggled into the pillows and pulled the covers up to her chin. The mattress felt soft enough to swallow her whole—she almost wished it could. She wanted today to be done so she could start over tomorrow. Even Mia had decided they hadn't seen a robbery, in spite of the fact that they absolutely, definitely saw one with their own eyes. Why had Mia changed her mind? The unfairness of it made Maddie want to throw pillows across the room.

"Let's add notes to our travelogue," Lulu said.

Miss Julia scrolled through pictures on her phone, from the bus to the lions to the gallery, to their dresses and the picture of the three of them posed outside the concert hall. They had stopped to take that one even though they were late. Lulu had insisted. Mia and Lulu chattered about perfect captions for each picture, and Miss Julia typed them in.

"We should take some photos of Maddie's sketches to add to the travelogue," Mia said, clearly trying to draw her into the project.

Maddie tried to smile, even though she was pretty sure she wasn't convincing anyone. "Maybe tomorrow."

Mom and Dad's voices drifted through the doorway. Soon they were in the room, full of energy the way they always were after a concert. Mom kicked off her stage heels. Mia and Lulu burst out, talking over each other.

"You'll never believe what happened today," Mia said.

"We saw a robbery!" Lulu stood up and bounced on the bed, singing what had become her theme song. "Glimmer girls to the rescue!"

"Whoa, whoa, slow down." Mom caught Lulu and cuddled into bed with the girls. "Let's start from the beginning."

"Good night, all," Miss Julia said, heading for the door. "I'll let the girls tell you about today, Gloria, but if you want to talk about it later, I'm all yours."

"Thanks, Julia. See you in a bit."

Lulu bounced while Dad joined them and everyone settled deeper into the bed.

"Okay, tell me," Mom said to Lulu.

"Maddie found this painting that she loved so much she wanted to look at it *twice*, but when we went back to look at it the second time, we saw someone steal it," Lulu said.

"We don't know he was stealing it for sure," Mia pointed out.

"And then Maddie ran after him and we ran after her and we all crashed into an orchestra," Lulu added.

"He *was* stealing the painting," Maddie insisted, more quietly than her sisters.

"I don't understand," Mom said. "Are you girls joking? You saw someone steal a painting?"

"I haven't heard any news about a stolen painting," Dad said.

"And you really knocked into an orchestra? Is everyone all right?" Mom said.

"Well, the cellist thinks her cello might not be all right, but no one could see any dents," Mia said.

"You knocked over a cello?" Mom asked, looking at each girl in turn. "You know how expensive and special instruments are, girls."

"And you know better than to be running in a museum," Dad added.

"But we saw a thief!" Maddie's cheeks burned. "No one listened to us about him. After we met with the museum director and Miss Julia gave him our information in case the cello was hurt, we left the museum and I saw him again—the thief. He was walking away with the painting, right down the street, and no one believed me."

"I know you saw someone who looked like a thief." Mia used air quotes around the last word, making Maddie's cheeks burn even hotter. "It's just that he couldn't have been an actual thief. Like I've been saying, there would have been alarms or something."

"The museum director wasn't worried," Lulu piped up.

"People don't just take paintings off the walls in museums and walk down the street with them," Maddie said. "Not as part of their ordinary job. He had to have been a thief."

"He was really far away, Maddie," Mia said. "Maybe he was someone else entirely. And how do you know the exact size of the package he was carrying? Could you really tell from so far away? Plus, it was windy, and it was hard to see anything with all the coats whipping and dust blowing around. Maybe it was just a trick of your eyes."

"It was pretty windy," Lulu said.

"See, Maddie? It's like that bobby told us yesterday. The first thing to do when you think you see a crime is to consider all the possibilities. What makes the most sense is that we saw something that *looked* like a robbery, but wasn't, since no one freaked out."

The longer Mia talked, the more Maddie's eyes filled with tears. She tried to blink them back, but they started running down her cheeks.

Mom looked from Maddie to Mia and back to Maddie again.

"Why's Maddie crying?" Lulu asked.

"You know what," Dad said. "I was thinking I'd tell you all a story."

"Great idea, Dad," Mom said. "Why don't you tell Mia and Lulu a story? Maddie and I will be right back."

Maddie climbed over Lulu and followed Mom out of the room, silently wiping the tears away. She knew she shouldn't be arguing with her sisters, but no one was listening to her or taking her seriously. Plus, she felt responsible for the painting, responsible for helping it find its way back to the purple room wall, where it should be. Even though she knew she might be overreacting, she couldn't stop herself.

"Come on over and sit down, Maddie," Mom said gently.

om moved pillows on the couch to make a little
nest for them and then found a box of tissues.
Maddie took one and pressed it against one eye and
then the other, soaking up her tears. Mom pulled her
close.

"Now, what's all this, sweet girl?" Mom asked.

"No one will listen to me," Maddie said. "I want to
talk about how important this is and no one is taking me
seriously."

"Well, I'm here and I'm listening," Mom said. "I want
to hear what you have to say."

"I know what I saw, Mom. Someone stole a painting
and I don't think anyone is even looking for the thief."

"What if what you saw . . ." Mom started, as though
she was weighing every word carefully. "What if it was
odd, but not a robbery?"

"You didn't see him, Mom. We watched him reach up
and take the most beautiful painting in the whole museum
off the wall. And he looked over his shoulder like he was
afraid someone might see. It seemed so suspicious."

"So, then what happened?"

Maddie pictured his retreating back as he'd hurried
through the employees-only door. "He went into an
employees-only door, and Mia wouldn't go in because

that would be breaking the rules. So we ran downstairs
to see if we could cut him off . . ."

"And that's when you ran into the cello?"

"It's not funny, Mom," Maddie said, catching the
smile in Mom's voice.

"I know it's not, sweet girl. But I can just imagine
the look on your face when you came around that corner, not expecting a cello, of all things."

"I know everyone wants me to let it go—Miss Julia
and Mia and the museum director. But then I saw him
later, walking away with a painting-sized package
wrapped in brown paper. That's not what happens with
famous paintings, is it?"

"Sweetheart, I don't want to argue with you about
this. Maybe you're right. Maybe you did see a robbery.
But don't you think news of a stolen painting would
have already been broadcast everywhere? Wouldn't
we have heard about a theft at a famous place like the
National Gallery and also about a citywide search for
the thief? Or if it was a theft, and somehow the museum
staff hasn't yet realized it happened, they still must
have security footage from cameras and access to inves-
tigators who can figure this out much better than we
can. It's not our job to find thieves."

Mom was trying to make her feel better, Maddie
knew, but she felt like everyone was *handling* her. No
one was taking her seriously. She pushed one finger
after another into the pillow on her lap, watching each
of the indentations slowly disappear.

"I just . . . I have to prove—"

"Maddie, unfortunately, I don't think we can prove anything. The man is gone, and we wouldn't be able to find him even if we tried."

"But, Mom . . ."

"Sweetheart, I don't want this to ruin your time in London. We're on a very special trip, and I want you to have fun. I don't want you to be filled up with worries, particularly when they're worries about something we can't fix."

"But what if there is something I can do?" Maddie asked.

Mom didn't respond for a moment, considering. "Is there something you think we might be able to do?"

Maddie scrolled around her mind for options, but came up blank. She couldn't think of a thing. Mom was right, but she still didn't feel right letting it go.

"People shouldn't get away with doing wrong things," Maddie insisted.

"You're right," Mom said. "You're absolutely right. When I watch the news or when I see situations that are definitely wrong, and that I can't fix, I feel very frustrated. I want to do something, but sometimes the solution is beyond my capability."

"So, what do you do?"

"I pray," Mom said. "I know praying sounds like a very small thing to do. And of course, God knows all about every situation without my telling him. But sometimes when I pray about things, God gives me ideas about ways that I *can* do something. Usually—almost always—what I can do turns up as a complete surprise."

"You think I should pray about the thief?"

"I think you should bring anything that's making your heart heavy and worried to God, and let him hold it for you. There's a passage in Philippians that says, 'Do not be anxious about anything, but in every situation, by prayer and petition, with thanksgiving, present your requests to God. And the peace of God, which transcends all understanding, will guard your hearts and your minds in Christ Jesus.'"

"Guard my heart from what?"

"From worry," Mom said. "Worry gets in our way. As soon as there's something we can do about the painting, if there's anything we can do, we'll do it. But until then, it's important to let go of worry. Do you see why?"

"Because then I'm not trusting God to work it out?"

"That's a big part of it," Mom said. "Would you like to pray about this right now?"

"I'm not really sure what to say," Maddie said.

"Remember, praying is just talking to God. You don't have to use fancy words. All you need to do is tell him what's on your mind. The way you'd tell a friend, or Mia, or me. Even though we can't see God, he wants to be as close to us as any friend would be."

"It feels a little weird sometimes, talking to God when I can't see him. When he doesn't talk back."

"We may not hear an actual voice," Mom said. "But that doesn't mean God doesn't talk to us. Sometimes God gives us answers by causing an idea to pop into our heads, and sometimes his answers actually do feel like words we can almost hear. Other times, we don't hear anything at all. That's when we have to trust the very most. We have to trust that prayer matters, even when we don't see results right away."

"I guess I'll try praying about this," Maddie said, not feeling very sure at all.

"Good girl," Mom said, kissing the top of her head. "I'm so proud of you, Maddie."

Maddie closed her eyes and tried to think of how she'd explain the problem to a friend. Slowly, the words started to come. "God, I think I saw a man steal a painting today. I got in trouble for chasing after him, and it didn't feel fair. No one listened to me. Well, except Mom. And I feel like I should do something more to help, but I don't know what to do. So, maybe that's what I want to ask . . . If there's something I can do, will you help me figure it out? And if there isn't . . . I guess . . . help me let it go. So that Mia and Lulu and Miss Julia and I can all have fun. And Mom and Dad too. And thank you for letting us come to London to stay in this amazing hotel and see art and everything. In Jesus' name, amen."

Maddie opened her eyes and looked at Mom. "Was that okay?"

"That was perfect," Mom said. "Do you feel any better?"

Maddie stared down at the pillow and considered. "Maybe a little bit."

"Do you want to go see if we can catch the end of Dad's story?" Mom asked, nodding toward the peals of laughter coming out of the girls' room. "Sounds like it's a good one."

Maddie grinned, realizing it had been hours since she'd truly smiled. "Let's go!" She led the way back to the bedroom, back to her sisters, leaving as much of her worry behind as she could.

EIGHTEEN

Early the next morning, the girls and Miss Julia ate toast and berries. Then they loaded up into a cab and were off to the Tower of London. They'd decided to take the first tour at nine a.m. so they'd also have time to watch the changing of the guard at Buckingham Palace.

"And we're really going to see crowns?" Lulu asked. "Real ones with jewels?"

"Yes," Miss Julia said, snapping a photo of Lulu's wide-eyed expression for the travelogue.

"Ones that kings and queens wore," Mia added. "I wish we could try them on. Do they ever take them out?"

"They use the crown jewels for coronations," Miss Julia said. "So, when a new king or queen is named, they take out pieces from the collection for the ceremony. The crown jewels aren't just crowns, either. We'll see scepters and swords and necklaces and bracelets, and some of the most famous diamonds in the world."

"I wonder if anyone will put my jewelry into glass boxes and look at them when I'm old," Mia said.

"What, because we're royalty?" Maddie teased, remembering Mom's story about Sir Robert Peel.

"Well, we are Glimmer girls," Mia said. "And that's nearly as good."

"As fun, at least," Maddie said.

"Glimmer girls, sparkle and shine!" Lulu shouted.

"Yes, but never leave out the most important part," Miss Julia said.

"But most of all, be kind!" the girls shouted in unison.

Maddie pushed all thoughts of being a detective out of her mind. Today, she had decided to have a fun day no matter what. Soon, the cab pulled up to the curb at the Tower of London, which turned out to be a castle, not just one tower. High stone walls surrounded the fortress, with a wide stone bridge leading up to an iron gate. Miss Julia paid their admission, and then they gathered with a small group to listen to a man wearing a top hat with a red band, and a black and red jacket.

"He's called a yeoman or Beefeater," Miss Julia whispered to the girls.

"What's that?" the yeoman asked. "Speak up, if you're going to speak at all. Well, actually, no. Don't speak. This group has paid top dollar for this tour, so we'll all keep our mouths shut and listen up. Got that?"

Maddie glanced over at Miss Julia, unsure whether they were really in trouble or if the man was joking. Miss Julia winked.

"Now, is anyone here from Australia?" the yeoman asked.

No one said anything.

"Now, now, speak up. Ignore what I said before," he said, cracking a smile. "How about anyone from America?"

A few people raised their hands, including Maddie, Mia, and Miss Julia. Lulu jumped up and down as she raised hers.

"Love to see that national spirit!" the yeoman said, indicating Lulu. "How about anyone from Europe?" he asked. "There's no one here from France, now, is there?"

No one raised a hand. Maddie caught Miss Julia's eye and grinned, happy to be in the know about at least something.

"Anyone from France?" he repeated, looking for any offenders. "Good."

Everyone laughed.

"Well, no matter where you're from, you're all welcome here at Her Majesty's Royal Palace and Fortress. My name is Thomas. I'll be taking you on a tour of the tower and telling you stories. Stories, ladies and gentlemen, but not necessarily the truth."

Everyone laughed.

Thomas, the yeoman, continued on, explaining the history of how the Tower was built. William the Conqueror defeated the Norman people, and they weren't happy about being defeated and having him as their ruler. He wanted a fortress to impress and dominate them. William's fortress started with the White Tower, which is part of the current Tower of London. Over time, other kings added to the fortress. Sometimes it has been a palace, other times it has been a prison, and the Tower of London was even bombed during World War II. But after the war, the damage was fixed so people could continue to tour the grounds and see the Tower of London as it had been hundreds of years ago.

After Thomas had talked enough to fill Maddie's head twice, he told everyone to follow him, and they crossed the bridge and went through the gates. Inside the outer wall, they found another wall made up of a number of buildings. Thomas explained that Sir Isaac Newton had lived and worked in one of those buildings.

"A very important man. He invented gravity, you know," Thomas said.

Mia nudged Maddie. They'd done a report together on Newton this year in school and had learned just about everything there was to know about gravity. Well, probably not everything there was to know, but a lot, anyway.

The group followed Thomas past the inner wall, where the tower grounds opened up to grassy grounds, and in the center, a stone tower.

"That's the White Tower," Thomas said. "Home of the Crown Jewels."

He led them around the Tower grounds a little longer and told story after story. Miss Julia clicked so many photos that Maddie stopped counting, and she let Lulu take a number of pictures too. Maddie liked the way Thomas joked while keeping a completely straight face. Then, when he did smile, it was like the sun coming out on a gray day. Whenever he smiled, she couldn't help smiling too.

At the end of the tour, Thomas led them into the White Tower so they could walk through and look at the jewels. Maddie had been looking forward to seeing the collection, but she hadn't expected to feel so . . . awestruck. Even Lulu whispered the entire time they were inside the White Tower. The jewels on the crowns and swords glimmered and glinted in the light. Maddie thought about the people who had worn them, people who had been crowned king or queen. What made someone special enough to be made a queen? In England, you became a king or queen because of your family. Even being in the Glimmer family, Maddie knew that just because you were part of a certain family didn't mean you were a certain kind of person. She may be able to get up and sing with her sisters and enjoy the feeling, but she couldn't imagine what it would feel like if she was expected to grow up and be a singer like Mom or a producer like Dad.

"Aren't they beautiful?" Lulu whispered, her nose only inches away from the glass.

"Yes," Maddie said, and then hugged her little sister tight. "Love you, Lulu."

Lulu looked up at her, surprised. "Love you too, Maddie."

"Are you girls ready to head over to Buckingham Palace?" Miss Julia asked. "If we go now, we should be able to find a spot where we can see the whole ceremony."

"Yes!" Lulu said, and then put her hands to her mouth, realizing how loud she'd spoken. "Yes," she repeated, this time in a whisper.

Maddie tried to keep her giggles as silent as she could until they were out on the Tower lawn.

Mia twirled around in a classic Lulu move. "I love London!"

Lulu and Maddie joined the dance and twirled and leapt their way toward Traitor's Gate.

NINETEEN

By 10:45, the girls and Miss Julia had found their way to Buckingham Palace. People stood three or four deep around the barricades, so they circled round until they were on the far side and better able to see the famous Changing of the Guard.

The guards stood in front of the palace, just outside little booths that looked almost like telephone booths, but were blue and black instead of red. Each one of the guards was unmoving, wearing a red jacket with gold buttons and a tight-fitting gold band around the collar, and holding a rifle. They wore tall, furry hats with gold bands that circled under their chins, covering up a lot of their face so what you could see most of all was their stern expression.

"Why do they just stand there, not moving?" Lulu asked.

"That's one of the most special things about the Queen's Guard," Miss Julia said. "They take their job very seriously, and as part of it, they stand still for hours."

"For the whole time they're in front of the palace? How long is that?" Mia asked.

"They have two to three hour shifts," Miss Julia said. "And they mostly stay still, but they are allowed to do ten-step marches every once in a while."

"But they never have to scratch their noses or anything?" Lulu asked.

Miss Julia laughed. "I think everyone's nose itches now and then."

"So they just ignore it? I could never do that," Mia said.

"I couldn't either," Maddie said.

"It would be very difficult, especially if people tried to make you laugh, the way people do with the Queen's Guard. But it's important to remember that the soldiers aren't just here for show. They're real soldiers—who fight in wars if they have to and everything else. This is only one of their duties, and a big honor. If something goes wrong, they will definitely move."

"Please take a picture for the travelogue," Lulu said. "We'll all stand here very still like soldiers so you can take it."

After what felt like forty tries, Miss Julia finally managed to take one picture where no one was smiling. Maddie didn't mind. So far, this picture had been the most fun one of the entire travelogue. When she finally stopped laughing, Maddie took out her sketchbook and drew one of the very still soldiers, stern face and all.

The crowd fell silent as far-off music started to play. Soon, Maddie could see the red jackets and gold hats, and the way the musicians stepped in perfect time as they played.

"Can you imagine trying to walk like that at the same time you were trying to play?" Mia asked.

"Crazy," Maddie answered.

Tubas and other brass instruments filled the air with sound, punctuated by the sharp staccato of drums and the repeated ring of cymbals. Ahead of the musicians marched the conductor, outfitted in a long gold jacket, using his long baton to keep everyone in time.

As the musicians assembled in the courtyard to continue playing, the new guards marched in, also in perfect step. Even though their bright red-and-gold uniforms, their tall hats, and perfect marching made them seem like toy soldiers come to life, Maddie knew Miss Julia was right. Those weren't toy rifles. Anyway, toy soldiers would have been modeled after the real thing, not the other way around.

One soldier marched ahead of the rest, shouting commands. To Maddie, these sounded like, "He-hup! Ha! Heffulump!" Probably not what the commander was saying. Up closer, and to the soldiers, surely these were clear orders. After another shout, the soldiers step-stepped, and then went still. They'd lined up with their backs to the girls, facing the courtyard. Another shout, and a few soldiers marched forward to face some of the current guards. They stood facing one another and then swapped places, the old guards now marching back to join the rest of the assembled soldiers.

"What do you think happens if one of them messes up?" Mia asked Maddie.

"It doesn't seem like they ever do, does it?" Maddie said. "I don't know, it all seems so serious. If it were me, I'd never be able to stop myself from laughing."

Maddie looked back at the Square and then froze. Her eyes narrowed. No. She couldn't be seeing what she thought. But yes, the more she looked, the more she was sure!

"What, Maddie?" Mia asked.

"I think I see him," Maddie said, up on her toes now, leaning this way and that, trying to see.

"Who?" Lulu asked. "Who, who?"

"The thief!" Maddie said.

"Where?" Lulu asked.

"What's going on, girls?" Miss Julia asked, turning away from the ceremony to give them her full attention.

"There, on the other side of the courtyard," Maddie said. "I can tell by the gray steaks in his hair, and those wire glasses. I'm pretty sure—"

"I'll catch him!" Lulu took off running, straight into the courtyard, and straight toward the lines of soldiers.

The next few moments seemed to happen in slow motion. Lulu's plan seemed to be to dart around the soldiers, on the straightest path possible to the thief, but instead of going around them, she knocked into the soldier on the end of the line, causing him to stumble and knock into the soldier beside him. Maddie and Mia watched in horror as guard after guard stumbled and scattered, black hats toppling everywhere, with Lulu in the middle of the whole mess.

"Oh no," Miss Julia said. "No, no, no!"

She gave Maddie and Mia her most serious look, ten times the one she'd given them in the museum the day before. "You two stay right here and don't move."

They both nodded in agreement, and Miss Julia hurried into the courtyard, making a beeline for Lulu.

TWENTY

Maddie bounced up and down on her toes, watching the thief move farther and farther away. "He's getting away!"

"Why are you so sure this guy is a thief?" Mia asked.

"You saw the same thing I did, Mia. Why *don't* you think so?"

"I don't know. Because no one else is worried, I guess. Because no one is talking about a stolen painting."

"Mia, I promised Mom I'd let it go, and all day, I have. But I prayed last night asking that if there was anything I could do, God would make it clear. And now I see this guy again, here. It's like I'm specifically being given another chance to follow him and find out what's going on."

"You mean, from God?" Mia's eyebrows raised skeptically.

"Could be." Maddie knew she was on shaky ground.

"I don't think God expects kids to chase down thieves."

"Okay, well, even if God didn't send him, what's the harm in following him and seeing where he goes and maybe who he is? I really, really need to know what happened yesterday."

"You are taking this whole thing too seriously," Mia said.

"If we go together, and we're careful, it will be fine. Come on, Mia. Please? Miss Julia will be upset for a second, and then she'll come along. Look, he's already made his way through the crowd. We'll never catch up with him if we don't go now."

"Okay, Maddie," Mia said. "If this is truly so important to you, then let's go catch this guy."

The two girls joined hands and started to run. Instead of battling through the crowd, they followed Lulu's lead and went straight across the courtyard, careful not to run into any guards.

They passed Miss Julia and shouted, "Come on!"

Miss Julia called after them, "Girls, wait!"

They were already on their way. Maddie glanced over her shoulder. Lulu and Miss Julia had untangled themselves from the pile of guards and were now running across the courtyard too. Satisfied that they were all together, if a little spread out, Maddie doubled her speed.

"Come on, Mia. He's turning the corner!"

Weaving in and around people, they ran and then walked whenever they got too close.

"What do we do if we catch him?" Mia asked, breathing hard.

"Let's just see where he goes," Maddie gasped. "Maybe we'll figure out where he lives or works or something when he stops. Then we can ask someone for help."

Maddie felt ridiculously conspicuous, but the man seemed unaware of being followed. He walked briskly on, down street after London street, past telephone booths and post boxes, old-fashioned lights, and window boxes filled with brightly colored flowers.

"What are you girls doing?" Miss Julia asked as she finally caught up with them.

"We're catching him, we're catching him!" Lulu shouted.

"Shhhh!" both Maddie and Mia hissed.

"You cannot follow a strange man through the streets of London," Miss Julia said.

"But he's a thief!" Maddie whispered.

"*Especially* if he's a criminal," Miss Julia said. "We need to leave this situation up to the police."

"We're keeping our distance. He has no idea we're following him," Maddie said. "And you're with us, so we're safe."

Mia pointed. "Look, he's turning onto another street!"

The girls hurried around the corner so they wouldn't lose sight of him. Miss Julia had no choice but to follow, grumbling under her breath. Now that Maddie was all-in, she knew she'd have to prove this guy was a thief, or face her parents' anger. The only way they'd forgive her for running Miss Julia all around town was if it was for a very, very good cause—such as saving a famous and beautiful painting. For one tiny moment, Maddie allowed herself to think about how she would feel once she found the painting and the thief was caught. Rather than being the one who was always last to join in, the one who never said the most interesting thing, the one just off-center, she'd be the one who'd spoken up and taken action.

The man turned one last corner, and headed up a set of stone steps into what looked like an office building. Trafalgar Square was just at the end of the street, and in the distance, Maddie could see the National Gallery.

"Look where we are!" Mia said.

"I know! This is the direction he was walking yesterday." Maddie held out her arm to stop everyone so they wouldn't get too close and be spotted.

Once the man was inside, she said, "Come on! Let's go see."

Miss Julia didn't say anything. She followed along silently, her lips pressed together in a thin line, as though she was holding back all the things she might say.

Mia and Maddie raced each other up the steps, with Lulu right at their heels. A sign above the door read, *National Archivist, Ltd.*

"Like the National Gallery?" Lulu asked, dancing around in excitement. "We found our thief!"

"But wait," Mia said. "An archivist is someone who takes care of paintings and documents and old things, right?"

"Yes . . ." Miss Julia said, her brow furrowing.

Maddie paused, less sure than she'd been all the way across town. If her thief worked here, maybe Mia had been right all along, and he hadn't been a thief at all.

"We should definitely go inside," Mia said, and Maddie knew she was doing the twin-thing, listening in on Maddie's thoughts. "We should ask questions and get to the bottom of what's going on here. You still want to know, right, Maddie?"

"Right," Maddie said, but her voice came out more like a question than a for-sure answer.

"Let's go!" Lulu said, and pushed through the doors before anyone could stop her.

Mia looped her arm through Maddie's, and they followed Lulu inside.

TWENTY-ONE

Inside the building, it was at least fifteen degrees colder and at least twice as dark as it had been on the streets outside. And it hadn't been warm or bright outside. Maddie's teeth started to chatter.

A dim desk lamp lit the receptionist's desk and cast grim shadows across her face as she looked up with surprise. "May I help you?"

Kids must not come here very often, Maddie realized. She looked at Lulu and then at Mia, but clearly, no one knew what to do next. They couldn't exactly demand to see the man with wire-rimmed glasses.

Miss Julia shot Maddie a *say-something* look. Seeing that no one was going to help her out, Maddie stepped up to the desk.

"We, uh, came to see the man who just came in."

"Mr. Hughes?"

"Yes," Maddie said, trying to sound sure when she was anything but.

"Do you have an appointment?" the receptionist asked, flipping through a book on her desk. "I'm afraid Mr. Hughes is quite a busy man."

Maddie fidgeted, trying to think of the right answer. Mia and Lulu always had something to say, but now, when she needed help . . . nothing? And shouldn't Miss

Julia say something? She thought of Miss Julia's expression when Lulu toppled the guards and the sound of her voice when she'd told the girls to come back. No. Miss Julia was definitely not going to smooth this over for Maddie right now.

"We don't have an appointment, but we really need to speak to him," Maddie said. "It's urgent."

The receptionist narrowed her eyes at Maddie, sizing her up, and then picked up the phone. "Your name?"

"Maddie Glimmer. And these are my sisters, Mia and Lulu."

She dialed and waited. "Mr. Hughes? I have three American children here to see you. Maddie, Mia, and Lulu Glimmer . . . No, sir, they did not . . . I'm not sure. They say it's urgent . . . Yes, sir . . ."

Maddie shifted from foot to foot, her discomfort growing. If Mr. Hughes was the thief, there was no way he'd want to talk to them. But he hadn't seen them at the museum, or when they'd been following him—at least she didn't think he had. Maybe he'd think they were harmless kids. But if he wasn't the thief, what reason would he have to talk to three kids he'd never heard of before?

"Yes, blonde hair, one is wearing a . . . They do have a guardian here with them. Okay, yes, sir, I'll send her right up." She hung up and spoke only to Miss Julia. "Mr. Hughes would like to see you, Miss . . . ?"

"Julia Twist," Miss Julia said, shooting Maddie a *this-is-going-to-stop-now* look.

"Mr. Hughes thought there might be a few blonde children following him today as he walked back from Buckingham Palace. He'd like a word with you."

"Of course," Miss Julia said.

"His office is up the stairs and to the left. The girls may have a seat on the bench over there and wait. I'll keep an eye on them."

Maddie, Mia, and Lulu sat. Lulu swung her legs, obviously not a bit bothered.

Mia elbowed Maddie. "Do you still think he's guilty?"

"I don't know," Maddie whispered, eyeing the receptionist.

"Maybe he won't talk to us because he *is* guilty," Lulu said, her voice loud and clear.

"Excuse me?" the receptionist asked.

"Nothing," the girls chimed in unison.

"I must ask that if you must speak at all, keep your voices down. This is a place of business, girls."

Good thing this receptionist wasn't their nanny. Miss Julia might get mad every once in a while, but at least she didn't wear her hair in a too-tight bun and have too-strict rules that even made something like waiting in a lobby uncomfortable.

Maddie tried not to talk, listening to the tic-tic-ticking of the clock. She rubbed her arms to keep warm.

"It's freezing in here," Lulu said to no one in particular. "Why don't you turn up the heat?"

The receptionist gave her a withering look. "We are an archival office. Cool temperatures keep the paintings and documents from deteriorating."

"So that's what you do here? Take care of old paintings and things?" Maddie asked.

"Yes," the receptionist said, deliberately looking away from them and back at her computer screen.

"Maybe we can get some clues from her!" Lulu whispered, and then raising her voice again, said, "Do you know of any paintings by Renoir?" She said Renoir with a strong "r" at the end.

"Ren-oir!" Mia corrected, pronouncing his name in the French way.

"Of course I know of Renoir," the receptionist said.

"There's this painting," Lulu said, jumping to her feet and slinking around the room, the way a detective might in a cartoon. "We call it 'Sun-Splattered Afternoon,' but that's not its real name. Anyway, it's missing from the National Gallery. And we think we know who took it!" At this, she turned and pointed her finger directly at the receptionist.

"Lulu!" Maddie said.

"Come sit down," Mia said.

"I'm going to have to insist that you girls stay quiet until Miss Twist returns. And that you stay seated," the receptionist added as an afterthought.

Lulu shrugged one shoulder and sat back down with her sisters. "I think she's guilty too. We'll see."

Even though the receptionist could clearly hear everything Lulu had said, she didn't respond.

"Girls?" Miss Julia had come down the stairs. "Mr. Hughes would like to speak with you for a moment."

Maddie shot the receptionist a triumphant look as she followed her sisters upstairs. The truth! She was finally going to get the truth. She would look Mr. Hughes in the eye and demand an explanation. Soon, the painting would be back on the wall of the National Gallery and it would be all because she, Maddie Glimmer, hadn't given up.

TWENTY-TWO

The stairway and upper hall were just as dim as the rest of the office. Shady. The kind of place where criminals might hang out. She'd been so busy chasing after Mr. Hughes, she hadn't thought of what she'd say to him when she found him. Mentally, she ran through her questions. *Why did you steal the painting? Where is it now?* If he denied being the one who took it, what would she say then?

The tightness around Miss Julia's mouth and eyes had relaxed, and her cheeks weren't flushed with frustration anymore. The meeting must not have gone the way she expected. Maddie wondered what that meant. Did Miss Julia finally believe her, now that she'd looked into Mr. Hughes' guilty face?

The office was surprisingly cozy, with overstuffed armchairs and a couch. Where outside, the dim light was bluish and cold, in here, the lampshades were amber, giving the room a warm glow. Even though the temperature wasn't any warmer, the room felt inviting, less like an industrial refrigerator.

"Come on in, girls," Mr. Hughes urged. "Now, sit yourselves down. It sounds as though we've had a bit of a misunderstanding."

Miss Julia introduced the girls to Mr. Hughes, and then she, Mia, and Lulu sat together on the couch. Maddie stayed on her feet, eyeing Mr. Hughes critically. Was the warm, welcoming tone his way of putting them off his criminal trail?

He perched on the edge of his desk, took off his glasses, polished them with a handkerchief, and then put them back on. "I have to admit, I was a tad concerned when I realized a parade of girls was following me back to the office after lunch. But then Miss Twist explained that you saw me remove the Renoir from the wall at the National Gallery, and all the pieces fell into place."

"So, you admit that you stole the painting?" Maddie demanded.

"Actually, I didn't steal it," Mr. Hughes said. "Are you sure you don't want to sit down?"

Maddie folded her arms. "I'll stand."

"Have it your way." Mr. Hughes cleared his throat, and then scanned the room as though someone might be hiding in the shadows. No one was, of course, and so he went on. "Now, girls, what I'm about to tell you is confidential."

"That means it's top, top secret!" Lulu said, starting to bounce on the couch. "I knew this was going to be good when I chased after you at Buckingham Palace."

"That's why all those guards knocked into one another today?" Mr. Hughes asked and then glanced at Miss Julia. "Oh dear, we seem to have made quite a mess, haven't we?"

"I didn't mean to knock into anyone," Lulu said. "There were so many of them, and they were in my way . . ." As Miss Julia caught her eye, her voice trailed off. "I'm really sorry about it."

"What's done is done. I didn't realize you girls were following me until I was quite a distance from Buckingham Palace. Turns out that you're rather good at following people. Not"—he raised a finger—"that I'm suggesting you follow anyone else. If you truly believe you've found a criminal, you should do exactly what your nanny has told you to do and tell a bobby."

"So, what's so confidential?" Maddie insisted, not willing to be distracted from what actually mattered.

"Here at our office, we keep a vault of valuable paintings when they aren't on display at the National Gallery."

"Why aren't all of the paintings on display?" Mia asked.

"We have far too many paintings to display all of them at one time." Mr. Hughes shook his head regretfully. "Honestly, many paintings which ought to be seen are languishing in our storage vaults. Most of those vaults are housed at the National Gallery itself, but when a painting needs special attention or restoration, we bring it here to our office."

Maddie felt like a teakettle about to boil. Mr. Hughes was acting so reasonable and as though he had all of the answers, but he hadn't explained the thing she wanted to understand. "But why did you take the Renoir off the wall, and then look over your shoulder like you hoped no one saw? We *saw* you," she said.

Even though his glasses were already spotless, Mr. Hughes took them off and rubbed them clean again before answering. Maddie wished she could be a tea-kettle and start to whistle, loud and long, until he got to the point and spilled the truth.

"The truth is," Mr. Hughes said, putting his glasses back on again, "we've had a string of robberies recently, all paintings that were newly brought here to the archives. The theory is that someone is watching which paintings we bring to the archives, identifying those that he or she wants to steal, and stealing them from us, here. Our security in this office isn't as tight as the security at the National Gallery."

"I don't understand," Maddie said. "If you need more security, why were you taking the painting all by yourself with no one else around?"

"We figured that by cutting out the procedures, paperwork, and official red tape, we might be able to avoid notice. Maybe that way, we could bring paint-ings here without the thief's knowledge. I scheduled my pickup of the painting to be just before the concert, when I thought no one would be around."

Mia frowned and then started to nod. "That's actu-ally a good idea! If the thief worked for the National

Gallery and was watching the paperwork to plan his robberies, he might not find out about the paintings until they were treated or repaired and back in the more secure vaults at the National Gallery."

"Exactly," Mr. Hughes said.

"But how do you know it's not someone who works *here*?" Mia asked.

"We've investigated all of our employees, plus we have a very small team. Everyone knows everyone else here, and we trust one another. We value the paintings, or else we would never do what we do—so much hard work for so very little money. No. No one here would ever steal a painting. The National Gallery, on the other hand, has an extensive staff. There are curators, administrative staff, security, even retail and wait staff, all of whom might have access to the employee-only areas. When someone clocks in or out, how hard would it be to slip into the office and take a look at the paperwork?"

"So you didn't steal the painting?" Maddie asked, the truth starting to settle in.

"No," Mr. Hughes said. "In fact, it's here in our back office. Would you girls like to see it?"

Mia sprang to her feet. "Would we?"

"Me too, me too!" Lulu said.

Maddie swallowed hard and shook her head. She'd run her sisters all over town, insisted she was right, refused to listen to Mia's common sense about how an alarm would for sure have gone off.

"You know what," Miss Julia said. "Why don't I wait here with Maddie? You girls can go see the painting with Mr. Hughes. But, Lulu?"

"What?" Lulu said, all innocence.

"No touching anything. That goes for you too, Mia."

"Got it," Mia said, grinning. "You sure you don't want to come, Maddie?"

Maddie shook her head again, not able to speak over the lump in her throat.

As soon as the girls left the office, Maddie sank into one of the chairs and buried her face in her knees.

TWENTY-THREE

iss Julia knelt beside her and rubbed her back.
"Oh, Maddie."

"I was so sure I was right," Maddie said. "So sure."

For a long time, Miss Julia stayed silent. Maddie pressed her forehead against her knees, trying to make sense of what Mr. Hughes had said. Finally, she sat up and shrugged at Miss Julia.

"I'm okay now," she said, speaking more to her knees than to Miss Julia. "Really."

Miss Julia put a hand on Maddie's arm. "You know, when I was about your age, I went into my classroom after lunch and found one of my friends—one of my best friends—in our classroom, looking guilty. I tried to figure out what she was doing in the room, but she wouldn't tell me. Later that day, our teacher, Ms. Hoy, sat us all down for a serious talk. Some money was missing from her purse. She asked if anyone knew what happened. I sat there, knowing I should say something about my friend, but I didn't. I told myself I didn't know what my friend was doing, that she could have been doing anything in the classroom by herself. The next day, my friend came to school with a new pair of earrings, the kind all of us girls were wearing that year. She'd been talking about wanting a pair of her own, but her mom wouldn't buy them for her. Maybe they were too expensive for her family to buy, I don't know. But the minute I saw those earrings in her ears, I knew that she'd bought them with Ms. Hoy's money. And I still didn't say anything. Maddie, being the kind of person who stands up for what's right is a good thing. You were brave, and you stood up to everyone because you wanted to do the right thing."

"But I wasn't right. Mr. Hughes isn't a thief."

Miss Julia smiled. "Even so, speaking up isn't easy. It takes courage. Do you remember how hard it was for you to sing on stage with your sisters just yesterday? And now look at you, facing down a criminal in his office!"

Maddie laughed, a hiccupy kind of laugh. "Not a criminal."

"You thought he was! And you stood there and faced him down. That's bold."

"I'm not like Mia and Lulu," Maddie said. "I'm never going to be the kind of girl who wants to stand on stage and perform like they do."

"No, but you're exactly the way *you* should be, Maddie," Miss Julia said.

Maddie shook her head. "I'm not any particular way."

Miss Julia looked her straight in the eye. "I know it's hard to see yourself from the outside. I feel that way a lot of the time too, Maddie. Just know that you're a special, brave girl, someone I admire."

Maddie could hear the honesty in Miss Julia's voice. Even though Miss Julia was saying such big, seemingly impossible things, she didn't seem to be saying them only to make Maddie feel better. Maddie dared looking up at Miss Julia's face, where she saw nothing but truth. She nodded slowly.

"Lip gloss?" Miss Julia said, so suddenly that she made Maddie laugh. Miss Julia rummaged around in her purse. "Lip gloss generally makes everything feel better."

Miss Julia never offered any of her makeup, not even when Lulu begged and begged.

Maddie put some on and couldn't help but smile at her reflection when Miss Julia held up a mirror. "Thanks, Miss Julia."

"Let's go find those sisters of yours," Miss Julia said. "Before a Glimmer burns down this office or something equally disastrous."

Maddie giggled all the way back to Mr. Hughes' office.

"Maddie, it was so amazing," Mia said.

"Thank you, Mr. Hughes, for giving us so much time this afternoon," Miss Julia said.

"It's my pleasure," he said. "And thank you for taking such an interest in our paintings. Now remember, no trailing after criminals, girls, do you hear?"

"Yes, sir!" Lulu said, saluting. "Are you wearing lip gloss, Maddie? I want some!"

"Come on, girls," Miss Julia said, winking at Maddie. "We can discuss lip gloss outside."

TWENTY-FOUR

D own the stairs they went. In the lobby, the receptionist glanced up with the same frown she'd worn
from the moment they walked in. She looked as though
she was about to say something, but stopped as a young
woman came out from the downstairs hallway. The
woman had paint under her fingernails and was carrying a large bag over her shoulder, the kind an artist
might use to carry a portfolio. She was mid-conversation
on her phone, but paused to say to the receptionist,
"Deliveries complete!"

"Thank you, Aria," the receptionist said.

Something was so familiar about this woman—the
receptionist had called her Aria. Maddie stared after
her, and then it clicked. Aria had been in the National
Gallery offices too. Maddie trailed her out onto the
steps in time to hear her say, "Yes, three o'clock, by the
fountain in Trafalgar Square."

Tossing Maddie an annoyed look as though she
realized Maddie had been eavesdropping, the woman
yanked the bag up on her shoulder and hurried away.

Maddie's heart thudded in her chest. Aria had been
talking about Renoir when she was at the National
Gallery, and now she had planned a suspicious-
sounding meeting. Plus, she was carrying a bag that

was plenty big enough to carry the painting. If Aria made deliveries to the National Gallery and to the National Archives, she had plenty of access to make it possible for her to pull off the robberies.

"Maddie, what now?" Mia asked as she walked up to her sister.

"I want to go see the painting," she said.

"Now?" Mia asked. "But you said—"

"I know. I changed my mind."

If the painting was missing, minutes after Lulu and Mia had seen it with their own eyes, someone would have had to have taken it in that very small window of time. If so, wouldn't that prove Aria had to be the thief? Maddie couldn't bring herself to tell anyone her suspicions, though, not after everything that had happened. What if she was wrong again?

"Maddie," Miss Julia said, in her most patient of voices. "I understand your wanting to see the painting now that you're feeling better, but we already took up a lot of Mr. Hughes' time. Maybe later I can call him and see if we can set up an appointment before we leave town."

"But I need to see the painting *now*," Maddie said.

"I'm sorry, Maddie," Miss Julia said. "I really don't want to disappoint you, but seeing the painting now isn't an option. I promise I'll call Mr. Hughes to set an appointment up for you."

"I'm hungry!" Lulu said.

"We're just around the corner from the hotel," Miss Julia said, checking her watch. "Your mom's concert is at three thirty today. We have a couple hours. Should we go eat some lunch and rest a bit before the concert?"

"Doritos for lunch!" Lulu shouted.

"And some vegetables," Miss Julia said, but she was smiling.

Mia hung back to walk with Maddie. "I'm sorry you didn't get to see the painting. But now you'll get a private showing of it with Mr. Hughes. You can look at it as long as you like, maybe sketch it, the way you wanted to."

Maddie couldn't stop thinking about Aria and her meeting. If she couldn't prove that the painting was missing right now, how else could she stop Aria from selling the painting? Because that was what was going to happen, Maddie was sure of it.

"Is the vault downstairs?" she asked Mia.

"What?" Mia asked.

"Did Mr. Hughes take you downstairs to go into the vault to see the painting?"

"Yes, why?"

"Are there a lot of locks? Is the painting in a safe?"

"There are not a lot of locks, no. Only a key card that Mr. Hughes used to go through a door, and the painting was right there, out on the table. He said they were going to do some tests to make sure the painting wasn't deteriorating."

"So if someone had a keycard, she could go in there and take the painting at any time?"

"I guess so. But didn't Mr. Hughes say that no one from their office would do something like that? They looked into everyone, I think."

"Yes, they checked all of their employees, but what about everyone who works at the National Gallery? They couldn't investigate all of them, because there are too many people. And what about delivery people, like that lady—Aria—who just left the office?"

"What about her?"

"She had a giant bag with her, big enough to hold a painting. How do we know she didn't just steal it right out from under our noses?"

"Don't you think enough is enough?" Mia rounded on Maddie, arms folded. "You've run us all over town. We all followed you even when we didn't think Mr. Hughes was a thief. We're in London, Maddie. Can't you just relax and have fun? Since when have you become obsessed with solving mysteries?"

"I'm not obsessed, I just want to know what's happening in this particular case, with this particular painting. I just . . . feel like I shouldn't let it go."

"What's going on back there, ladies?" Miss Julia asked, giving Mia a warning look. "You know, I think we're all pretty tired. Maybe we can talk more about what happened today—if we need to—after lunch. For now, I think we should put the subject away."

Maddie stuffed her hands into her pockets and kept walking, trying to think of a solution. If she couldn't talk about the robbery, and she only had until three o'clock today to do something about it, what options did that leave?

God, she prayed silently, *help me figure out what to do*.

Was it truly her responsibility to do anything at all? As soon as the question popped into her mind, she pushed away the thought. Of course it was. She was the only one who had all the pieces. That meant she was the only one who could stop "Sun-Splattered Afternoon" from being sold to who-knows-who. Somehow, in some way, she would be there at Trafalgar Square today at three o'clock.

TWENTY-FIVE

Back at the hotel, they sat at a glass-topped table in the lobby restaurant and had tomato soup and grilled cheese sandwiches for lunch. Lulu also ordered Doritos, and Miss Julia ordered a side of English peas, which turned out to be surprisingly sweet and tasty. Maddie tried to enjoy lunch, tried to enjoy listening to her sisters joke and laugh, but the clock kept tugging at her attention. Minute after minute ticked by. 1:45. Then, 1:55. How long did it take to walk to Trafalgar Square from their hotel? Not long—they'd done it the first day they came to London, on their way to tea.

She couldn't ask Miss Julia to go with her, but surely Mia would go along. Lulu would definitely be up for the adventure, but she'd never be able to keep the trip a secret from Miss Julia. For that matter, Maddie had no idea how *she* could keep the trip a secret from Miss Julia.

"I think we should all take a power nap before the concert," Miss Julia announced, looking over at Maddie with concern. "We've had so much excitement today. The Tower and the Palace, and then our cross-London hike. Plus, we were up very early, and I know you girls are a little jet-lagged still."

"I don't like naps," Lulu complained, and promptly yawned.

"How about we all curl up in our beds then," Miss Julia suggested. "You can read or do some other quiet activity. If you nap, great. If not, no big deal."

Maddie tried to act casual as they headed off to their rooms, but inside, she was doing a happy dance. Here was her opportunity to slip away from Miss Julia with Mia! All they had to do now was to wait out Lulu, until she fell asleep, and then they could go. Lulu would be furious when she found out they'd gone without her, but Maddie knew they couldn't get halfway to the door with Lulu in tow. Even if she was trying to sneak, she'd most likely sneak full volume.

They snuggled under blankets and Maddie pretended to read, flipping page after page but not taking in a word. 2:05. 2:08. Finally, she heard Lulu give a tiny snore—her little sister was asleep.

"Mia!" she whispered.

Mia blinked over at her, obviously halfway to sleep herself. "Huh?"

"Mia, you know that woman we saw leaving Mr. Hughes' office? I think she's the thief."

"Wha . . . ?"

"She's meeting someone at Trafalgar Square at three o'clock, and she's going to sell the Renoir painting. You know how I said I needed to see it? That was because I had to prove that the painting was stolen after you all looked at it. But no one would let me. So now, my only option is going to Trafalgar Square to see for myself."

Mia's eyes went huge. "You want to sneak out—just us—and go to Trafalgar Square, because you have another wild idea? No way. Absolutely no way, Maddie."

"Come on, Mia, please? I need your help."

"Go to sleep, Maddie," Mia said. "When you wake up, hopefully you'll be back to your normal self. Miss Julia is right, you're too tired to think straight."

"I am not too tired, Mia."

But Mia was clearly finished with the conversation. She turned onto her side, away from Maddie, and closed her eyes.

Maddie watched Mia lay there until she drifted off to sleep. Lulu was still fast asleep and now, so was Mia. Probably Miss Julia was too. Maddie checked the clock again. 2:27. If she was going to go, now was the time.

Slowly, and as carefully as she could, so as not to knock into Mia and wake her, Maddie climbed out of bed. She pulled on her tennis shoes and snuck out into the main room. She'd thrown her coat over a chair, so she put that on. Then, she scanned the room, wondering what else she should take. A room key, probably, but she didn't have one of those. She'd have to worry about getting back into the room later. Maybe one of the hotel staff people would help her. She'd probably have to fess up about sneaking out, but after she'd caught the thief—for real this time—no one would be mad, would they?

Well, actually, yes. Everyone would be mad. Mom, Dad, Miss Julia, even Mia. And especially Lulu, since she'd missed all the fun. 2:31. Now. Maddie had to go now. At the last minute, she remembered her cell phone, the one she was supposed to use only for emergencies. The phone was in her bag with her sketchbook, which she'd left on the coffee table. She tiptoed across the tiled entryway, carefully opened the door, and closed it behind her. Standing still in the hallway, she counted to twenty, sure that Miss Julia would burst out of the door any second and demand to know what Maddie thought she was doing. Nineteen, twenty . . . Nothing.

Maddie looked back at the door, and then squared her shoulders. She could do this. She had to, because it was the only way to save "Sun-Splattered Afternoon."

TWENTY-SIX

No one stopped Maddie on her way out of the hotel. But then, no one knew she was doing anything wrong. The doorman even opened the door for her and tipped his hat.

The first thing Maddie noticed once she was outside was all the noise. Car engines, horns honking, people talking, the sound of the wind blustering through the trees. When she was with her sisters, everyone was so busy talking that she never noticed any of these things. She shoved her hands into her pockets and kept her eyes down. She could make it to Trafalgar Square in time—she knew she could.

"Excuse me," a woman said, sounding mildly offended.

Maddie looked up, heart racing, sure she'd been caught. The woman staring her down wore her gray hair swept up into a bun, and a miniature poodle pranced this way and that at her feet.

"Watch where you're going!" the woman scolded.

"Oh, sorry," Maddie said. "Excuse me."

"Kids these days," the woman said, huffing as she went on her way.

Maddie watched her go, then counted to twenty again, willing her heart to slow down. *Breathe, Maddie.*

You're fine. No one knows you're not supposed to be out here.

She looked up, gauging the distance to Trafalgar Square. It was not far away at all. Certainly, she could be there in ten minutes, five even, and she could be near the fountain, ready to see everything that happened between Aria and whomever it was she planned to meet.

Maddie took a deep breath and continued. The block seemed longer than any city block she'd ever walked. Surely, everyone was staring at her. When a bobby rode past on his horse, she ducked into the shadow of some steps, as though the shadows would hide her from sight. The bobby rode on, not paying her any mind. Watching him go, Maddie blinked, her understanding of the world tilting slightly on end. She'd never realized how easy it would be to sneak out and be out on her own. She'd always thought everyone would know she wasn't allowed. But different families had different rules, of course. Lots of kids could be out on their own for various reasons.

Maddie thought about how it would feel to have parents who let you run around on your own when you were only ten years old. She and Mia always complained that there were way too many rules in her family, but on second thought, maybe they had the just-right amount. Not that Maddie regretted coming out here—she had to do this thing—but she wouldn't want it to be no big deal that she was out on her own. Because, in truth, it felt like a very big deal.

She passed through the gates with the giant lions and wove her way through the crowds of people toward the fountain. Now what? She didn't want to stand out in the open, right next to the fountain, especially since Aria had seen her earlier. There wasn't a bench where she could sit and be inconspicuous, either. Maddie turned in a full circle, taking in the wide open square. She could maybe sit on the steps, but they were so far away, she'd hardly be able to see anything at all.

What now, God? she prayed, hoping some very clear answer would pop into her mind. Nothing. She wasn't all that surprised. Honestly, she wasn't sure being out here on her own was what God wanted her to be doing right now. If she was really, truly honest with herself, she had to admit that Mia was right. God didn't expect kids to chase down thieves. This definitely hadn't been what Mom meant when she said God might give her something to do. Maybe she'd handled this all wrong, but no one had listened to her. And she felt out of options, cornered, even. All she wanted was to find "Sun-Splattered Afternoon" and prove . . . yes, prove that she hadn't been entirely wrong.

Why did she need to prove herself? Mia would definitely demand Maddie's answer on this question. Maddie had no answer. She didn't seem to be able to stop herself. She was like a boulder that had started rolling and kept picking up speed, unstoppable until it made it to the bottom of the hill. Or crashed into something.

Maddie looked around at the other people, trying to figure out a look-casual strategy. People were either walking, or standing still, staring into their phones. That was it! All she had to do was take out her phone and pretend to be reading it, or taking pictures or something, and then no one would think it was weird that a ten-year-old was standing on her own in the middle of the square.

After fishing her phone out of her purse, Maddie turned the power on and flipped through screens. She had a few games, but not much else on her phone. Really, it was meant to be for emergencies. Still, no one else had to know she wasn't reading important messages on the glowing screen. She positioned herself about thirty yards away from the fountain, where she could see most of the way around. If the woman ended up on the exact opposite side, Maddie figured she could move around slowly, making sure not to miss anything.

Her phone read 2:55. Just in time.

TWENTY-SEVEN

As the clock ticked off minute after slow minute, Maddie flinched at every tiny sound. Three o'clock came and went, and Maddie still didn't see Aria. Slowly, Maddie began to circle the fountain, starting to doubt herself. What if she'd heard Aria's conversation wrong? What if there was no meeting at all?

Then, just as she was about to turn around and head home, Maddie saw Aria approaching the fountain, still carrying her large bag. Aria scanned the crowd warily. Maddie ducked behind a tall man so she wasn't in direct sight. Wow! She was not so bad at this detective stuff. Mia would be proud. Maddie grinned, and then remembered to focus. Aria's meeting. The painting.

Maddie sidestepped, as casually as she could, until she had a clear view of Aria. She checked her watch and then scanned the crowd again. This time, Aria seemed to see whomever she was looking for. Then, Maddie saw him too, a man in a perfectly pressed suit, with two giant men following him, men that made Mom's security guards look like the Scarecrow from *The Wizard of Oz*. The three men strode across the square to meet Aria.

Once they arrived, Aria and the perfect-suit man began to talk. Maddie couldn't hear what they were

saying, far away as she was, but she imagined what
might be happening.

Do you have my painting? the man might be asking.

Yes, it's right here. Aria indicated her bag. *Did you
bring payment?*

Painting first.

Payment first.

Are you going to keep wasting my time?

Maddie realized she was narrating this conversation
as though it were a television show, as though whatever
happened didn't really matter. But this wasn't a television show, and what happened mattered quite a lot.
"Sun-Splattered Afternoon" was at stake. Maddie had
meant to stop the meeting, but now that she was here,
she realized stopping the meeting wasn't as simple
as she'd thought. How was she supposed to inter-
rupt a man and his two security guards—or whatever
they were—who were breaking the law and buying a
painting that wasn't officially for sale? Not by running
up and saying, "Excuse me, can you please stop that
right now?"

Maddie flexed and clenched her fingers, thinking,
digging through her mind for any workable solution.
Meanwhile, the man had nodded to one of his guards,
and the guard had opened up a briefcase to show
the woman whatever was inside. After Aria checked
the contents and nodded, the guard closed the briefcase again. Then, Aria took a painting-shaped parcel

wrapped in brown paper out of her bag. The man ripped open a small corner to look at the painting. He nodded too.

No, no, no! Maddie couldn't just stand here watching, but her body felt as immovable as if she were one of the bronze lions guarding the Square. What had she been thinking? It had been one thing to think she was coming over to confront Aria, but now, she realized she was witnessing a real crime. One she had no idea how to handle. Out of the depths of her mind, the bobby's words sprung to mind. *I'd call for backup.* Backup! She whirled around, looking for a bobby. It had seemed as though there had been bobbies here and there and everywhere this whole trip, and now, Trafalgar Square was completely bobby-free. *No, no, no, no, no!*

The guard handed over the suitcase and Aria turned to go. As the man and his guards began walking away, Maddie bit her lip. Should she follow Aria or the man? If she followed the man, she'd stay with the painting, but it wasn't like she could stop him and his guards. She'd need the police for that. But Maddie thought maybe she'd be brave enough to face Aria down. Or maybe as she followed Aria, she'd run into a bobby along the way. At least she could ask Aria who the man was, and why she'd stolen the painting. Hopefully, from there, the authorities could find the man and recover the painting.

Now that she had a plan, Maddie was able to move again. She shoved her phone into her purse and began to weave her way through the crowd, keeping Aria in sight. Aria seemed to sense that something was wrong, because she started to jog. Maddie glanced over her shoulder to see if the man had changed his course, but he was nowhere in sight.

"Oof!" Maddie said.

"Watch where you're . . . Maddie?" a man's voice said, one that sounded particularly familiar.

Of all people, Maddie had run directly into Mr. Hughes.

"Oh, Mr. Hughes. Mr. Hughes!"

"Maddie, what in the world are you doing out here on your own? Where's Miss Twist? And your sisters?"

"I just saw . . . the painting . . . you have to . . ." Maddie grabbed Mr. Hughes' arm and pulled him in the direction Aria had just gone.

"Maddie, slow down," Mr. Hughes said. "Tell me what's happening."

Maddie took a deep breath, and tried to calm down enough to explain, keeping her eyes on Aria's retreating back. "She stole the Renoir! And she's getting away!"

"How did you know the Renoir was missing?" Mr. Hughes asked, his eyes going round.

"I just knew. And I promise to explain, Mr. Hughes, but we have to go, right now, or we'll lose her."

"Well, yes, yes of course," Mr. Hughes said. "Lead the way."

TWENTY-EIGHT

Maddie took off running after Aria with Mr. Hughes pounding down the pavement behind her. Something had clearly spooked Aria, because now she was running full-out.

"You're . . . quite . . . the runner," Mr. Hughes gasped.

"She's turning the corner!" Maddie called.

Sure enough, they'd lost sight of Aria. Maddie's heart sank, but she kept running, hoping that when they made it to the end of the block, Aria would be somewhere they could see her. There. Her head bobbed as she ran, far ahead of them, past a few groups of walking people.

Down street after street, around corner after corner, Maddie and Mr. Hughes slowly closed the distance. Maddie's legs ached and her lungs burned, and she started to wonder if she'd have to give up, when they finally rounded one last corner to catch sight of Aria climbing a set of steps up to a door.

"But that's Aria," Mr. Hughes said, as he caught sight of the woman for the first time. "She delivers all of our mail from the National Gallery. And she . . . Oh!"

He looked over at Maddie in amazement. "How in the world did you know?"

Maddie pulled Mr. Hughes out of sight as Aria checked over her shoulder, scanning the street. She must not have seen them, because she went inside and closed the door. Maddie doubled over, catching her breath.

When she finally could breathe again, she said, "I saw her at the National Gallery. She was talking on the phone about a Renoir, which caught my attention, because we'd just seen you take the Renoir. I thought her talking about a Renoir meant everyone knew about the robbery, but then the director didn't know anything about what had happened."

"And he didn't explain our new procedure for bringing paintings to the Archival office, since that procedure is confidential," Mr. Hughes said, nodding. "I see."

"The director treated me like I was crazy, and didn't tell me anything at all," Maddie said. "I noticed Aria in the first place because she had paint under her fingernails, the way my art teacher at school does. I've always thought that I'd know I'm a real artist when I have paint under my fingernails like that. You know, the kind that doesn't come out no matter how hard you try, because every time it's almost gone you paint again and cake more on."

"You're an artist?" Mr. Hughes asked.

"I draw, and sometimes I paint."

Mr. Hughes looked about to say something more when something caught his eye and he looked over Maddie's shoulder and seemed to remember they were

standing on a random street outside Aria's house, and
that she had just stolen and sold a painting. "So . . . back
to the point. How did you know Aria was the thief? And
how did you know she'd be at Trafalgar Square today?"

"I saw her at your office earlier. She was on the
phone again, talking to someone about meeting at the
Square at three o'clock, and that *it* would be ready.
After she'd been talking about the Renoir, I had this
feeling I couldn't ignore, not even when I knew I should
let it go. And you said the thief had to be someone who
knew which paintings had come to your office. Since
she was a messenger, Aria could poke around in both
offices. Plus, she had a giant bag that could easily have
hidden the painting. I asked Miss Julia to let me check
if the painting was missing, but she said we couldn't
bother you."

"And if you'd come back in, we might have been
able to stop Aria from selling the painting."

"But now it's gone. She sold it to a man with two
huge guards."

"We can work on finding him later. But for now,
I suppose we need to go speak to Aria." Mr. Hughes
started toward Aria's house and then stopped. "What
am I thinking? Actually, what we need to do is to get
you home."

"But we can't let Aria go!" Maddie said. "She ran all
the way home—she might have even seen us following
her. She won't wait around long."

"No one knows you're out here on your own, true?" Mr. Hughes asked, and then answered his own question. "Of course that's true. The minute someone realizes you're gone, trouble and lots and lots of worry are going to break out. They've probably already discovered you are gone. Do you have any way to contact Miss Twist? Her phone number, perhaps?"

A few blocks down, a bobby clip-clopped across the street on his horse.

"Officer!" Mr. Hughes called, but the bobby didn't turn back.

"I have my emergency phone," Maddie said. "But it's only for emergencies . . ."

"I think this qualifies. Stay right here and call Miss Twist. I'll go down the block to see if I can catch that bobby." He gave her a piercing look. "Promise me you'll stay right there. I'm not going so far that you won't be in clear sight. I'll know if you take one step toward that flat. Got it?"

"Got it," Maddie said.

Her phone was heavy in her hands. She could already hear Miss Julia's voice on the other side of the phone, shocked, disappointed, angry. Maddie breathed deep and dialed. As the phone rang, Mr. Hughes came jogging back down the block, this time with the bobby in tow. The sight of Mr. Hughes running next to the sleek horse and its stern rider might have made Maddie laugh before, but not now, not while she waited for Miss Julia to pick up the phone.

"ello?" came a groggy voice on the other end of the line.

"Miss Julia," Maddie said.

"Maddie?" Miss Julia was immediately awake. "Is this your emergency phone? You know you're not supposed to . . . Where are you?"

Maddie heard rustling and shuffling, probably Miss Julia tossing off her covers, on her way to check the girls' room.

"I'm with Mr. Hughes," Maddie blurted out as quickly as she could, hoping she'd said it before Miss Julia saw the room for herself, before she saw that Maddie was not lying next to Mia where she was supposed to be.

"What's happening?" Mia's voice asked in the background. "Where's Maddie?" and then "Oh no!"

"Oh no, what? Maddie, where are you? This isn't a funny joke!"

"What joke?" Lulu piped up.

"I'm with Mr. Hughes. On . . ." Maddie read the nearest street sign. "Jasper Avenue. There's a bobby here too," she added quickly.

"You're not in the hotel room?" Miss Julia asked, her voice raising in pitch until it was so shrill it made Maddie's ears ring.

Maddie had known she would be in trouble, but she hadn't expected it to be quite like this. Her stomach tied itself into knot after knot until she felt like she might be sick.

"I want to speak to Mr. Hughes," Miss Julia demanded.

Maddie handed the phone over, relieved not to be the one on the spot anymore.

"Hello?" Mr. Hughes said. "Yes, she's here and she's safe. She ran directly into me in Trafalgar Square. Oh, no, no, I had no idea . . . Yes, I know, and I think . . ." Mr. Hughes eyed Maddie's face. "I think she knows too. But listen, Miss Twist, the thing is that Maddie found our art thief. Aria was under our noses all along—one of our delivery staff. We're just outside her flat now with a bobby."

He waited a little longer, listening.

"Yes. We're at 1335 Jasper Street. As soon as you're here, ring the bell. Yes, we'll keep Maddie with us, never out of our sight. I promise."

As he hung up and handed over the phone, the bobby was also hanging up his phone. "I've called for backup, but I've been cleared to go in on my own if the thief is unlikely to resist arrest. We don't want to give her time to escape, which may be the more pressing possibility."

"I thought I knew Aria," Mr. Hughes said. "But obviously, I didn't. That said, I'm sure she isn't a violent person. She may run, but I don't think she will resist arrest."

"You may come with me, then, to help me identify her. If there's the slightest hint of any trouble, I expect you and the girl to leave the flat, no questions asked," the bobby said, hitching his horse to the nearest lamppost.

"Got it," Mr. Hughes said, and in spite of her nervous stomach, Maddie smiled at the echo of the conversation she and Mr. Hughes had just moments before. The chain of command was clear, and now the bobby was in charge.

"This way," he said, marching up the stairs to the flat.

Rather than ringing Aria's buzzer, he rang another tenant and told them he was a police officer. "Please buzz us in. We need access to another tenant's flat."

The door clicked open and they hurried into the foyer. Straight ahead, a brass number one hung on the door.

"Number three must be on the third floor," the bobby said. "Let's head on up."

He led the way, and soon they were standing outside flat number three. "Ready?" he asked.

"Ready," Mr. Hughes and Maddie both whispered.

He banged on the door. "Open up, by order of Her Majesty's Metropolitan Police."

No answer. Maddie held her breath. She'd done just about everything wrong, and she was in miles and miles of trouble. If only one thing could go right, and she could know for sure that Aria would be stopped. If Aria had seen Maddie following her, Maddie would have been the reason Aria had run before she could be caught. If so, Aria's escape would be Maddie's fault too.

"I'll be opening your door in three," the bobby said. "One . . . two . . ."

The door swung open. Aria stood there a little behind the door, not willing to step forward.

Aria's eyes were wide, her face terribly pale. "What . . . How . . . ?"

"I'm afraid we must come in," the bobby said, not waiting for her answer.

Aria took a step back, and then another. She had no living room furniture, only easels, tarps, and art materials. A number of half-finished paintings ringed the room. One looked especially familiar.

"That looks like 'Sun-Splattered Afternoon'!" Maddie said, pointing.

"I'm sorry, who are you?" Aria said, frowning at Maddie. Then her eyes sparked with recognition. "You're the girl who I saw at the Archive—" She broke off, realizing she shouldn't say more.

"Aria, how could you?" Mr. Hughes said. "You're an artist. You know the value of paintings—"

"How could I what?" Aria asked, but her heart didn't seem to be in her words. She clearly knew she was caught.

She glanced over her shoulder, as though she was looking for somewhere to run.

"I wouldn't go anywhere, if I were you," the bobby said.

"How could you steal paintings that belonged to the people of England and sell them for your own gain?" Mr. Hughes pushed.

"Not for my own gain," Aria said, gesturing around her flat. "Look at this flat. Do I look like I live in luxury?"

"For what, then?"

Aria eyed Maddie, and then sighed, a deep, full-body sigh. Oddly, it didn't seem to Maddie that Aria was angry about having been caught. In fact, she seemed almost relieved.

"You'll find all the money in my safe," Aria said, gesturing to the wall. "I've never been able to spend even a penny of it. Couldn't bear to."

"If you weren't stealing the paintings for the money, what then?" Mr. Hughes asked.

"Keep in mind that anything you say may be used against you in court," the bobby said, clipping handcuffs on Aria. "I arrest you in the Queen's name as being concerned in the theft and sale of artwork which belongs to the National Gallery."

THIRTY

As though she hadn't heard the bobby, Aria pushed on, turning to Mr. Hughes. "Why did it take you so long to figure out what was happening?"

"I . . . It . . ." Taken aback, Mr. Hughes stumbled to find words. "Well, it was Maddie who figured it out, actually, in the end."

"I just wanted to be seen," Aria said. "I stole painting after painting, and no one even noticed."

Mr. Hughes looked completely taken aback by this. "We noticed paintings were being taken, of course! We just didn't know . . ."

"Do you know what it feels like to be an artist?" Aria demanded, stepping toward Mr. Hughes, even though the bobby had a firm grasp on her hands behind her back. "You spend hours and hours, weeks, months, years even, creating something beautiful. You put your creation out into the world and what happens? Nothing. Not one thing. No one notices. No one cares. Or, if you're lucky, someone notices but they tear you and your work apart. We're supposed to feel grateful that an expert paid our work a moment's attention, someone who has probably never lifted a paintbrush in his whole life. We're supposed to be grateful for his feedback, even when he stomps our hearts into the ground."

"But if you're an artist, you know how priceless a painting can be, how irreplaceable," Mr. Hughes said.

"A painting is simply an object, one that can be owned, bought, and sold, but we treat some like they matter and others like they're dirt. Sounds like the way we treat people, doesn't it?" Aria's eyes glittered, her face dark with hatred.

"So, this was only about making a point? You stole and sold priceless paintings, and will probably go to jail forever to prove . . . what?"

Aria didn't answer. Silence filled the room.

"To prove that every person matters," Maddie said, the words cold and frightening to speak out loud. Cold and frightening because she understood them, heard the same words echoing in her own heart.

"Yes." Aria slumped back against the police officer, no longer straining against her handcuffs. "Yes, that's exactly it."

"Let's go," the bobby said to Aria. "Where are your keys? We'll lock up your flat for now."

The hatred had already faded from Aria's face, but now her cheeks went truly pale. She looked around her flat, at all of her unfinished work.

Maddie crossed the room to look at the painting that looked like "Sun-Splattered Afternoon." "How did you get so much done on this, when you just stole the painting today? And how could you sell it before you were finished?"

"When you don't finish something, you never know what it can become. It still has all of its potential." Aria nodded to her keys sitting on a table and the bobby picked them up. "I always work on them quickly like that, just an hour or two to see how far I can get . . ."

Maddie circled slowly, taking in the other canvases. They were all beautiful—unfinished, but still beautiful.

"You stole all of these?" Maddie asked.

"It's a terrible loss to the National Gallery." Mr. Hughes shook his head. "To the people of Britain, in fact. We will certainly try to recover them. On that note, how do we handle the money in the safe?" he asked the bobby.

"First, after a thorough investigation, of course, she will have to stand trial. Once she is convicted, the judge will determine to whom the money belongs. But I'm relatively sure the money will be given to the National Gallery to help recoup losses."

"So, we're finished here?" Mr. Hughes asked.

"Yes," the bobby said.

"Let's go, then, Maddie," Mr. Hughes said. "You can lead the way."

Maddie passed Aria, and then stopped to look the young woman directly in her eyes. "If you can paint other people's paintings like that, I know you could paint your own. They'd be beautiful. I'd want to see them, anyway."

"There won't be any painting, I'm afraid," the bobby said. "Not for quite some time."

"Someday, then," Maddie said, and then more urgently, "Don't forget, no matter what happens."

They left the flat, down the two flights of stairs and out onto the stone stoop. Once they were outside, the bobby asked Mr. Hughes for his phone number and called to reroute his backup to the station. Then he untied his horse, but didn't mount. Instead, he walked with Aria on one side, the horse on the other, down toward the main thoroughfare.

"Thank you again for all of your help!" he called.

Maddie and Mr. Hughes waved, and Maddie felt as though she was waving to Aria just as much as to the bobby. As the two turned the corner, Maddie sank down onto the stoop.

"I suppose we should wait here for Miss Twist," Mr. Hughes said.

"Okay." Maddie wrapped her arms around her knees and pulled them tight. As she laid her cheek on her knees, she realized she was sitting almost exactly as Mary Magdalene sat in the painting in the green room at the National Gallery. Right now, Maddie wouldn't be able to put her thoughts into words if she tried, but maybe Mary couldn't have either.

THIRTY-ONE

After pacing up and down the stairs for a few minutes, Mr. Hughes sat next to Maddie. For a long moment, neither spoke. Maddie took her sketchbook out of her bag and started to draw. Aria's high cheekbones, her shoulder-length hair, long bangs swept across her brow. Her eyes, the way they'd looked when Maddie had told her not to forget to paint—sad and surprised too.

"May I?" Mr. Hughes asked, motioning for the sketchbook. "I'd love to see your drawings."

Usually, Maddie would never share her art with someone she didn't know well, but somehow, she didn't mind showing Mr. Hughes. She passed it over. After he looked at the drawing of Aria, he flipped backward through the pages and studied a few of the other images.

"You've got nice control of your lines," he said. "And your perspective and scale are strong too. How old are you?"

"Ten," Maddie said.

"Ten." Mr. Hughes shook his head. "I was about ten when I decided I wanted to be a professional artist when I grew up."

"You're an artist too?" Maddie asked, surprised.

"Nope. Not too far along the way, I realized I didn't have the drive," Mr. Hughes said. "If I had the choice to draw or to read, I'd read. Or spend time with friends. Instead of becoming an artist myself, I got as close to art as I could without having to make it myself."

"But don't you ever feel like something's missing? Like if you made something special, or did something important . . ." Her voice trailed off. She realized she was talking more about herself than about Mr. Hughes.

He handed back her sketchbook. "The way I see it, tending to art is a very important job too. In many ways, I agree with Aria. When people create a piece of art, they put a piece of themselves out into the world in visual form. Each artwork helps us see the world with new perspective—through that artists's eyes. By tending that artwork, I feel as though I'm telling each of those artists that their work matters. Maybe I'm not able to look them in the eyes to tell them so, but still, we honor each artist by caring for their work faithfully over the years. I suppose what I'm saying is that no matter what part you play, it's important that you play *your* part."

"Aria said it was like putting her heart out into the world and having it stomped on."

"Not everyone will see the world the way we do," Mr. Hughes said. "But I'd rather preserve the visions of many, rather than destroy them. Aria was thinking only of herself, of what the world would think—or not think—of her. She wanted people to pay attention to her, personally, and she was willing to do whatever it took to make that happen. But what will become of those paintings, scattered all over the world, in need of tending?"

"Whatever it took . . ." Maddie repeated. "I guess it's easy to become carried away and forget about right and wrong along the way, when you're so sure it will turn out right in the end."

"Such as sneaking out of your hotel on your own? Or chasing criminals across London?" Mr. Hughes asked, his eyes twinkling.

"Yes, such as those things," Maddie said. *"And knocking over a cello."*

"Plus half of the London Guard?"

Maddie raised her hands in innocence. "That was Lulu, not me."

Mr. Hughes laughed. "Right. Sorry."

"Honestly, I thought it would feel different to find the thief," Maddie said. "Aria will be locked up for years now, right? And she won't be able to paint. And the paintings are still missing . . ."

"But you tended to an artist," Mr. Hughes said. "You don't realize it, probably, but you did. Aria wanted to be caught, wanted to stop stealing paintings—I could hear that in every word she said. And you not only helped stop her stealing-spree, you reminded her who she truly is, an artist. That's not a small gift, Maddie."

"It feels small."

"Many times, it's the small things that add up over time that make the most difference," Mr. Hughes said. "Ah, Miss Twist!"

He stood to meet Miss Julia, who was hurrying up the block, Mia and Lulu in tow.

"Maddie Glimmer!" Miss Julia said, and then more softly, sweeping Maddie into a hug. "Oh, Maddie, I'm so glad you're all right."

Then, holding her at arm's length so she could look into her eyes, she asked, "What in the world did you think you were doing, wandering all over London on your own? Do you have any idea how far away you are from the hotel?"

"This last bit, the part from Trafalgar Square to here, she was with me," Mr. Hughes pointed out, trying to be helpful.

"Still!"

"Right," Mr. Hughes said, nodding. "Still."

"You snuck out and you didn't invite me?" Lulu wailed.

"I'm sorry, Lulu," Maddie said, trying to give her a hug, but Lulu would have none of it.

She went to stand on Miss Julia's other side and glared.

"Mia?" Maddie said, concerned that her twin hadn't said anything at all.

Mia eyed Maddie as though she was a stranger.

"We should go," Miss Julia said. "Thank you for taking care of her, Mr. Hughes."

As they started walking home, Miss Julia called Mom. "Yes, Gloria, she's here with us now. No, I don't think you should leave your concert. Well, if you think . . . Okay. Yes. We'll see you at home."

The walk home was quiet and terribly uncomfortable. Mia kept her silence and Lulu pouted. Miss Julia kept her hand firmly on Maddie's back, which Maddie knew was supposed to be a comfort, but which felt like a warning. What did she think? That Maddie was going to run off right now for no reason? Maddie wanted to tell everyone about catching Aria, but no one seemed to want to know. So much for doing something special. As soon as they reached the hotel, Maddie went to the girls' room and curled up on the bed, relieved to be away from her sisters and all of their anger. Relief quickly faded as she realized the only thing to do now was to wait for Mom and Dad.

THIRTY-TWO

When the hotel door clicked open, Lulu and Mia's feet pounded down the hall, both running to tell Mom and Dad what had happened.

"Maddie ran away!" Lulu said. "All the way across London!"

"She thought she could catch that thief," Mia said. "I told her not to sneak out, and she did it anyway after I fell asleep."

"And she didn't even take me!" Lulu wailed.

"Maddie? Maddie? Where are you?" Dad called.

"MADDIE?" Mom shouted.

Maddie looked up as the door to her room swung open.

"Maddie!" Mom strode into the room.

"What happened?" Dad demanded.

"You know better!" Mom said. "How could you sneak out of this hotel, away from Miss Julia, all on your own?"

Maddie curled more tightly into a ball, trying to block out Mom's anger.

"Oh, sweetheart," Mom said to Maddie, her voice softening. It was quiet for a moment, and even though Maddie had her eyes squeezed tightly shut, she knew Mom must be patting Dad on the shoulder, the way she sometimes did. "Why don't you give us a little one-on-one girl time?"

"I'll be with Mia and Lulu in the living room," Dad said.

Maddie heard him close the door and then Mom was on the bed, pulling Maddie into her arms. "Okay, so what happened?"

Maddie couldn't answer, not while every single person in her family was furious with her.

"I shouldn't have yelled," Mom said, her voice soft now, and soothing. "I'm sorry, Maddie. I was so scared when I heard you were somewhere out there on your own. I want you to be safe, always. I can't stand the thought of you being in danger. Let's start again, okay? Start from the beginning and tell me what happened."

Maddie took a deep breath. "You really want to know?"

"Yes, I truly do."

Hugging a pillow tight, Maddie sat with her legs crisscrossed and steeled herself to tell the whole story. She started with the palace, the knocking-over of the guards, the chase, and Mr. Hughes' office. Then she told Mom about Aria, and the overheard conversation.

"I knew it was wrong not to tell Miss Julia about wanting to go to the Square, but I also knew she wouldn't let me go. So I tried to convince Mia to sneak out with me. She wouldn't, and then I felt like I had to go on my own. It was like this boulder that started rolling and it kept picking up speed, faster and faster, until I was doing things that I didn't even want to do." Maddie shuddered. "I hated being out on the street alone."

"I can imagine," Mom said. "So, after you made it to Trafalgar Square, then what?"

"I saw Aria sell the painting to a man. He had two guards with him. I think that's when I started to realize how wrong it was for me to try to stop her all by myself. All along, I kept telling myself that maybe God wanted me to follow Aria. After all the clues that led to her, I thought maybe it was my special mission to stop her. But when I saw those guys and realized how serious the situation was, I knew I hadn't been listening at all. I just wanted to catch the thief on my own."

Maddie told Mom about running into Mr. Hughes, and about following Aria and catching her in her flat.

"I don't understand why you took this so personally, Maddie. What was it about the painting that was so important to you?"

"It wasn't the painting, really." Maddie smoothed out the pillow in her lap, trying to find the words to tell Mom as much of the truth as she could. "It was that I saw something wrong had happened, and I wanted to make it right. And I guess I wanted to do something special. I was . . . looking for my glimmer."

Mom smiled and pulled her close. "And do you think you found it?"

"I think so, maybe. I'm not sure how to put it into words. But I think it has something to do with drawing, with the way I can see into people when I'm drawing. And how that seeing can help me help others. Like the way I hopefully helped Aria."

Mom nodded. "Maddie, you should never have left. Sneaking out was very wrong. But I understand that you felt like no one was listening to you. And you helped catch the thief, right? I'm proud of you for your very great courage. Even in the middle of mistakes, God brings beauty."

"That's nearly what Mr. Hughes said, but he said it in different words," Maddie said.

"What did Mr. Hughes say?" Mom asked.

"After we caught Aria, she told us why she was stealing paintings—because she wanted to be special and get noticed. She's an artist, and people weren't paying attention to her, so she decided to start stealing paintings instead. I realized I was doing a similar thing—not stealing paintings, but acting like rules didn't matter as long as things turned out the way I wanted them to in the end. After the bobby took Aria away, Mr. Hughes talked about Aria wanting to be caught. She didn't want to be a thief—she wanted to be an artist. I think for her, the whole situation was a little like an out-of-control boulder too. Her paintings were beautiful and I told her so, and Mr. Hughes said that was a small but important thing to say, that sometimes the small things matter the most."

"I agree with him," Mom said. "I'll bet that Aria will remember what you said, and even while she's going through this hard time, God can use your words to help her. You showed her what it means to be a Glimmer girl. Even though Aria was stealing, you showed kindness to her."

"I'm sorry, Mom," Maddie said. "You even left your concert early, didn't you?"

"Nothing is more important than my girls," Mom said, putting her hands on Maddie's knees. "Of course, you understand that you will have a consequence. Dad and I will talk about that. But I want you to know that we forgive you and we know you'll learn from this."

"Lulu and Mia are still angry with me," Maddie said. "I want to make it right with them, and with Miss Julia too."

Mom nodded. "That is a tough one, but I think the best thing to do is to face it head-on. Maybe we can talk with your sisters over ice cream? What do you think?"

Maddie smiled a slow smile. "Okay. I'll go talk to Miss Julia now."

When Maddie had finished talking to Miss Julia, she came into the living room, where Dad was entertaining everyone with a snappy rendition of "This Little Light of Mine."

"Dad's working on our song," Mia said, obviously forgetting for a moment to give Maddie the silent treatment.

"Can I hear it?" Maddie asked, trying not to think about having to actually sing the song onstage and just enjoy the moment.

"Why don't we hear one round of it, and then ice cream for all," Mom said.

Dad started back at the beginning, and by the end, Mia, Mom, Lulu, and even Maddie were dancing and singing along. Maybe she still had some explaining to do, but she could see that things would be okay in the end. *Please, God. Help me have great courage, the way Mom said,* Maddie prayed, as they went out in search of an ice cream parlor.

THIRTY-THREE

I want a double-decker cone," Lulu said, pointing out the ice cream flavors she'd chosen. "With chocolate fudge and mint chocolate chip."

"May I have a cup with two scoops, Mom?" Mia asked.

"Yes, this afternoon, we're having the works. Ice cream before dinner, even," Mom said.

Mia ordered chocolate peanut butter and vanilla bean, and Maddie chose just one scoop of mint chocolate chip in a cup. She would save it until after the hard part was over, so she could really enjoy it.

The girls found a table, and Mia and Lulu sat opposite Mom and Maddie. Lulu dug into her ice cream right away, but Mia held off, watching Mom.

"Can we talk about what happened now?" Mia asked.

"Yes," Mom said. "I think it's time to talk."

"What I don't understand is why Maddie isn't in tons of trouble. I mean, she snuck out. Across London. And here she is eating ice cream."

"You're right, Mia," Mom said. "Sneaking out was very wrong. And Dad and I will talk about a fair consequence. But remember, we aim for consequences that fit the situation. Maddie has already faced some pretty tough consequences today, so I think a little ice cream is okay. I'll let her tell you about the day, and you can see for yourself."

Maddie told the story again, about how she felt like every last person was staring at her as she walked down the London streets, and then about watching Aria sell the painting and not being able to do a thing about it. She explained how she'd run into Mr. Hughes, and then the chase to Aria's flat.

"Just like our chase earlier today," Lulu said. "But faster and farther. I wish I was there!"

"I was only thinking about solving the mystery." Maddie poked her ice cream with her spoon, but still didn't take a bite. "I didn't think about what it would feel like to watch Aria be arrested. The bobby clipped handcuffs on her and walked her out of her house, probably to go to jail for a very long time.

"I also didn't think about how it would feel to be out in London without you two," Maddie said. "The whole time, I wanted you there with me. Mia, I knew you'd have a better idea what to do when Aria was selling the painting. Maybe if you'd been there, you could have helped me. And Lulu, I know you would have made the whole thing more fun. But the truth is, none of us really should have been there today. I should have told Mr. Hughes about Aria somehow, and then left it up to him. I thought I was trying to do everything I could to get someone to listen to me. Now I see that I could have tried harder. I could have thought more about asking for help instead of trying to do everything on my own."

"You know what I think?" Mom said, putting an arm around Maddie. "I think that even though Maddie did some very wrong things today, she was also very brave. She stood up against what she knew was wrong, and she helped Mr. Hughes and the National Gallery. I have a feeling that the Renoir will be found very soon."

"I'm sorry, Mia," Maddie said. "When you said we shouldn't sneak out, I should have listened to you. I should have figured out something else, like waking up Miss Julia or calling Mr. Hughes, or something. And Lulu, I'm sorry I hurt your feelings."

"I wish the Glimmer girls could have solved the case together," Lulu said. "It would have been our very first real case."

"I think we did solve the case together," Maddie said. "How would we have found Mr. Hughes' office if you hadn't charged into all of those guards at Buckingham Palace?"

"Charged into . . . what?" Mom asked.

"Ummmm," Mia said, jumping in quickly. "They all brushed themselves off and were fine."

"Anyway," Maddie said, pushing on, relieved that Mom was smiling, despite the fact they hadn't answered her question. "If Lulu hadn't done that, and Mia, if you hadn't chased after Mr. Hughes with me the first time, we'd never have found the office, and I'd never have overheard Aria. So, really, we all did solve the case together."

"Glimmer girls to the rescue!" Lulu shouted, and then clapped her hands over her mouth as everyone in the parlor turned to stare. "Oops!"

"Will you forgive me?" Maddie asked.

"Yes, of course." Mia smiled and took her first bite of ice cream. "Mmmm."

"Me too!" Lulu's next bite was so giant she nearly couldn't fit the spoon into her mouth.

"Watch out, you'll get brain freeze," Mom said, laughing.

Maddie grinned and took her first bite too. The minty-creamy taste was delicious, and even more delicious because she knew that everything would be okay now. Maybe even Aria would be okay in the end.

"What do you say we finish up and then invite Dad and Miss Julia to come with us to ride the London Eye?" Mom asked.

"What's that?" Mia asked.

"The giant Ferris wheel," Mom said. "It's not like any Ferris wheel we've ever ridden though. We'll all be able to go inside a capsule, ride together, and see the sights of the city. If we go now, we will probably be able to see the sunset!"

"Yay, yay, yay!" Lulu cheered, taking her very last bite.

Maddie took another bite of ice cream, letting the coldness melt in her mouth. Mr. Hughes was right— sometimes the small things did matter most of all.

THIRTY-FOUR

The London Eye was giant, as far as Ferris wheels went. It towered above them as they walked through the entrance gates. Dad paid their entrance fees.

Miss Julia eyed it doubtfully. "You know, maybe I should wait for you down here."

"Nonsense," Dad said. "You can't miss seeing all the sights of London from way up top. Plus, it's sunset. It's the perfect time of day to go."

Lulu could hardly stand still, she was so excited. "We'll see Big Ben . . ."

"We see Big Ben from nearly everywhere we go in London," Mia said.

"And the palace, and the Tower of London . . ."

"We already saw both those places up close," Mia said.

"And now we'll see them from up top!" Lulu said. "Like we're birds. Or dragons!"

They lined up to wait for their turn. The cars came around and moved so slowly they didn't even stop as the new people walked on.

"Whoa," Lulu said as she watched. "Awesome!"

"What's wrong, Miss Julia?" Maddie asked, noticing that she was hanging back.

"I'm just not . . . Well, heights aren't my favorite," Miss Julia admitted.

"The Ferris wheel moves very slowly," Maddie pointed out. "And you can take lots of pictures for the travelogue."

"You're right, of course," Miss Julia said.

"I was afraid out on the London streets all by myself," Maddie said.

"As you should have been," Miss Julia pointed out, giving Maddie a warning eyebrow.

"Yes. But I found out that something happens when you're afraid and you do something anyway."

"What's that?"

"You realize that the feeling—being afraid—doesn't have to stop you. You can take one step and then another and then another. And suddenly, you're doing the thing you thought you couldn't do."

Miss Julia blinked at Maddie, and then pulled her into a sideways hug. "And you think that will work for me?"

"I do," Maddie said.

"Okay, then," Miss Julia said. "It can't hurt to give it a try."

"It's our turn," Dad called over his shoulder. "Everyone into this next car."

Maddie took Miss Julia's hand. "I'll stay right here with you."

They stepped on and walked out to the edge. Slowly, slowly, the cars started to rise. Gold, pink, and red streaked the sky, and lights shone from the windows of the tall buildings.

"Do you think any stars will come out while we ride?" Mia asked.

"If one does, it will be the first star of the night," Dad said. "A wishing star."

"I know what my wish will be," Lulu said, leaping and giving a twirl.

Miss Julia shuddered. "How can she jump and dance and not hold on?"

Maddie squeezed Miss Julia's hand. So far, she was doing pretty well, though they were standing pretty far back from the window, far enough that she didn't have to see all the way down to the ground directly under them.

Up and up they went, and as they did, Miss Julia's hand started to relax. Eventually, she let go, and put her arm over Maddie's shoulder as they watched the sunset colors deepen.

"A star, a star!" Lulu said.

Everyone looked up. Maddie saw it, winking directly above them. She closed her eyes and thought about what she wished most of all.

I wish I will be the kind of brave that helps other people be brave too. That I'm brave in small ways that add up to something special. And that I'm brave enough to be Maddie, even if that's not all fireworks and leading the charge.

"What did you wish, Maddie?" Mia asked.

"You can't tell your wish," Lulu said. "Or it won't come true."

Mia linked her arm through Maddie's. "Well, whatever your wish, I hope it comes true."

"You too," Maddie said, and then linked her other arm through Lulu's. "And yours too, Lulu."

Miss Julia snapped a photo of the girls, with the London skyline behind them. Mom and Dad joined them, hugging all of the girls close.

"Here's to our last day in London tomorrow," Dad said. "Let's make it even better than today."

"And here's to all of our brave, clever, kind girls," Mom said.

"Like our motto says," Mia said.

"Glimmer girls, sparkle and shine, but most of all, be kind!" the three girls chorused.

Everyone laughed, and then turned back to the window to watch as their capsule slowly lowered back toward the ground.

Dolphin Wish

*By Award-Winning Recording
Artist Natalie Grant*

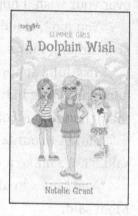

Join twins Mia and Maddie and their
sidekick little sister, Lulu, as they travel
the country finding adventure, mystery,
and sometimes mischief along the way.
Together with their famous mother,
singer Gloria Glimmer, and their slightly
wacky nanny Miss Julia, the sisters learn lessons about being
good friends, telling the truth, and a whole lot more.

In *A Dolphin Wish* — a three-night stop in the city of San Diego
seems like it might be just the break the girls need — lovely
weather and great sights to see. That is until they hear animal
handlers at Captain Swashbuckler's Adventure Park talking
about the trouble they've been having keeping the animals in
their habitats. Mia and her sisters cannot resist a challenge and
they talk Miss Julia into another visit to the educational amuse-
ment park to search for clues as to what or who is helping the
animals escape.

Available in stores and online!

Printed in the USA
CPSIA information can be obtained
at www.ICGtesting.com
LVHW032347230124
769797LV00038B/1464